ALL YOUR COLORS

Book One

Kylie R. Trask

ISBN-13: 9798371401809
ISBN-10: 1477123456

Cover design and art by: Kylie R. Trask
Library of Congress Control Number: 2018675309
Printed in the United States of America

CONTENTS

To finding soulmates in unexpected places. Whether platonic or romantic. And, if you are lucky- both.

This book is dedicated to mine which I was lucky enough to find.

First, Ray-
I love you with my entire soul for always believing in me.

Second, Joy and Isaac-
You came out of the blue when I needed you most. Forever grateful for such dear friends to share this journey with. I love you.

CHAPTER ONE

Marlee

"I'm gonna be late!"

Marlee— the overachieving nerd who never missed a chance at extra credit. Was late. She had always been on top of her game and was always at least ten minutes early to every class or function. So, the sight of her fumbling with her keys while trying to balance a backpack on her shoulder, a water bottle, and two books in her hands, was a rather amusing sight. She made a frustrated growling noise in her throat.

Ada, Marlee's roommate stretched her legs as she pulled one foot back toward her butt, then the other. Her ashy blonde curls were barely contained in a messy bun as her brows furrowed.

"Your class doesn't start for another thirty minutes, Mar."

"Yeah, but," She blew out a frustrated breath, trying to gesture with her whole body since her hands were full. "It takes me at least fifteen minutes to get across the entire campus to the theater building, and if the elevator is already in use, that could eat up to five minutes— *and* now I've been talking to you too long! I gotta go!"

She barged out of the door and ran down the hallway— barely hearing Ada call after her, "Don't forget we are meeting August at Pizzarini!"

She didn't call back but pinned the information into her mental calendar as the elevator opened like a miracle. She tried to keep her books in her arms as she ran.

"Move it peeps!" She bellowed, pushing through a group of girls.

Somehow making it into the elevator, she bumped the button with her water bottle. The clanging sound echoed around the small space. She bounced on her heels as it lurched down to the first floor of the dormitory, glancing at the girl who was riding down with her. They exchanged awkward smiles right before the doors opened and Marlee darted out.

She yelled out rushed 'hellos' to friends and acquaintances who tried to catch her as she sped across campus. And as she passed the coffee cart, Sanjay threw up his hands.

She half-yelled and half-whined, "I'm late, bro!"

Marlee loved her coffee, and it was a well-known fact that when she didn't have her morning shot of caffeine, the girl was, well, a beast. Sanjay gasped as he handed another student a coffee.

"Heathen!" he laughed after her.

She grinned, shaking her head as she rounded the corner. Sanjay had been one of her first friends outside of her dormmate when she started going to college. He was always laughing and was considered 'one of the girls' because he would have movie nights with her and Ada, and even participate in face masks. He also made the best cookies.

The theater was finally in sight, but Marlee didn't let herself slow down or even sigh in relief. She moved faster, bursting through the double doors like a stormy southern wind. Dropping her things in a clattering heap in one corner, she waved her, now free, arm.

"I'm here, I'm here!" Her voice came out breathless, wobbling on each syllable as much as Marlee did on her feet.

Blowing her tawny, brown hair from her face, she tried to paste on her usual 'I have everything under control' smile but, really, she just looked frazzled to the few students that were actually on time.

"Glad you made it?" One of the girls, Hannah, laughed.

The tall blonde was part of the cast for Beauty and the Beast, which Marlee was in charge of directing. And while Marlee didn't dislike the girl, she wouldn't deny that she was not one of her favorites to work with. Hannah had gunned for the lead at auditions but didn't get the part.

Understandably, she had been upset. But the girl had taken it out on Marlee, complaining that the choice of performing Beauty and the Beast was a little too *high school* for her. Of course, she hadn't told her, the director, but Marlee had heard these things from another girl who was also not a big fan of

Hannah.

Drama aside, she didn't care too much about all of that. The only opinion that mattered to her was that of the scout, rumored to be in attendance. As long as the cast and crew she had hand selected could pull off her vision, they could gossip all they wanted. Marlee looked around at the small group and then at her watch.

7:00 am.

She frowned. "Where is everyone? We are supposed to be splitting into groups to run lines and I need my set crew to meet with me in five to go over designs."

Bennet, who would be her lead as the Beast, stepped up beside her as the others shrugged and started to flip through their scripts.

"There was a big party last night. I think everyone is just a little late," he offered.

"And a lot hungover, most likely," Marlee grumbled.

He looked like he was biting back a smile, but she ignored him and flipped through her very organized and very highlighted director's binder.

"Go pair up with the others and start running lines together while we wait for the rest of our crew."

He nodded and left to round up the others. She was so glad there was at least one competent person around.

"Marlee?"

"Mhm?" She hummed, not looking up at the owner of the voice as she read over the list of students that *should* be present.

"The set design crew is wondering where to set up their shop?"

Marlee looked up at the girl talking to her. She blinked and pursed her lips, trying to remember her name.

Reagan, yes, that's it!

She smiled, but it faltered when she realized what Reagan had said.

"What? Where are they?" She spun around in a circle.

"Backstage—"

The girl didn't finish her sentence before Marlee marched off to find the design crew. She hadn't even met most of them since they were a group of art majors who weren't usually involved in the productions put on by the college. She thought they would have at least come into the auditorium and introduced themselves. Weaving through a hallway and up some stairs, she made it into the backstage area where, sure enough, there was a group of people milling around.

"If everyone back here is part of my set design crew, I'm gonna need y'all to move back into the auditorium," she announced, waving an arm back the way she came.

She tried not to outwardly cringe at how rude and bossy she sounded.

Maybe being two minutes late for my coffee would have been worth it...

"You want the art supplies in the auditorium?" One of the group members asked, brushing her vibrant pink hair away from her face.

Marlee started to nod but then shook her head. "No. You can leave the supplies here, but I need everyone in the auditorium for a quick brief on what is expected."

People started moving toward the auditorium and Marlee breathed a small sigh as she hugged her binder to her chest. Watching each of the students that passed, she tried to memorize the details of each face. She was bad at names, so this was her way of remembering each person she would oversee in the coming months.

Following them into the auditorium, she clapped her hands together. It looked like the rest of the cast had arrived and had split into groups to run lines as she had suggested to Bennet. She had been up most of the night prepping for today while her classmates had been partying. And she tried not to hold that against them because at least they were all here now.

"Okay," she started to say to the group of art majors, pulling out a stack of rough sketches from her binder.

She moved to a table set out at the front of the room and laid them out.

"These are some of the concepts I came up with for a few of the major scenes. Creativity is accepted here, so don't be afraid to hit me up with all of your ideas."

She took a breath and laughed, "I'm not an artist so, forgive my lack of execution, but I listed out a color scheme and some themes I am comfortable discussing." She looked around at the team of artists who nodded.

"Questions?"

The girl with pink hair nodded. "Yeah— Where is Mr.

Emery?"

Marlee blinked.

The drama teacher had informed her that he would be the teacher in the loosest form. He had told her he would check in and be watching her progress from the outside. She wasn't sure where he was today.

"Uh, I'm not sure, but he made me director for the entire production, so if you can't find him, I'm here."

This seemed to satiate them, so Marlee moved on to marking attendance as she made her rounds introducing herself to those she didn't know. The list was almost all marked off, but there was one name left.

She looked around the room again, frowning as she mumbled to herself, "Jericho Byers?"

As if on cue, the doors to the auditorium opened and he appeared. Almost an hour late. A few of his fellow art majors moved to greet him and he shifted his bag on his broad shoulder. She studied the wrinkled black and gray button-up and the paint-stained tee he wore. His dark, chocolate-brown hair hid most of his face, but the gauges in his ears peeked out as he bent his head to talk to his friend.

Snapping the binder closed, she pushed her round, metal-framed glasses back up her nose. She had no time for laziness in her own life and could barely tolerate it in other people. His friend pointed her way and some of her annoyance melted away into nerves when he turned to look at her. He looked utterly unimpressed.

Touche.

As he approached, her eyes caught first on the moth tattoo that fit perfectly over the front of his neck. She blinked up at his green eyes which reminded her of seafoam— *even though, technically, seafoam isn't green.*

At least, she didn't think it was.

"You're late."

She hadn't meant that to be the first thing she said to him, but the frustration with his tardiness had been escalated by the bored slope of his shoulders as he stuffed a hand into his pocket. She did feel a little embarrassed that she hadn't introduced herself before snapping at him.

He blinked, giving a small shake of his head.

"I'm sorry, and you are?"

"The director," she replied, brushing some of the shorter layers of her dark hair back behind her ear that burned at the edge.

She tried not to fidget with her jumper when he looked her over.

"Not Mr. Emery, then."

"No shit, Sherlock," Marlee said dryly.

Opening her binder again she marked him tardy and pointed her pen back at his friends.

"They can fill you in on what you missed. I'm kind of busy."

He held up his hands, his dark brows rising but he didn't say anything else as he turned to walk away. She was very glad about that. Jericho Byers might be the only thorn in her side so far, but she wasn't going to let her guard down. Marlee didn't plan on being easy on him. Or the rest of the cast and crew, for that matter.

She needed this show to be perfect.

CHAPTER TWO

Jericho

Jericho flipped through the sample designs and color schemes again. He sighed. Not only had he been roped into being a part of the school production, but his peers had elected him as their representative. Which meant he was in charge. And that meant he was the one who would have to work with the grumpy girl who was directing.

So much fun.

Not that it was particularly challenging. After all, he was known for being prickly. He could deal. And he could definitely match that energy. But that didn't make it less annoying.

He shook his head at the papers. "I'm not feeling inspiration from any of these." Lena brushed her pink hair out of her eyes, folding her arms as she looked at Jericho.

"Then draw up something else and check it with the director."

Jericho set the pile of papers down. "Yeah, that's not gonna go over well," he mumbled.

Lena snorted, "Are you scared of her or something?"

"No."

"Okay."

She sounded like she didn't believe him.

Jericho's eyes squinted just a little as he looked at Lena. With a sigh, he messed with the papers again, "Does anyone else have any ideas?"

"She said she was open to creativity," Lena commented, ignoring the question.

Jericho glanced back at the director whose nose was still buried in her binder. Even if she was, he doubted that she would take it well from him. She had been visibly irritated with him for being late and hadn't even introduced herself formally.

Grabbing up one of the papers he sighed through his nose and started to sketch his own ideas for the set. Perhaps he could amend her first impression of him by putting his heart into the work. He took one of the color schemes the director had given them, took the first two colors, and then the last two of a different swatch and paper-clipped it to the sketch.

It didn't take him long to put together an idea that he was happy with. Picking it up, he turned it around to show Lena who had been watching him put the vision together. She gave a nod with an impressed, downturned smile.

Jericho stood, brushing his hair away from his face as he approached the director. He paused a foot away and waited. She turned the pages of her binder, scribbling on some of the pages.

Wondering if she was purposely ignoring him, he rocked on his heels as he tried to decide if he should just walk away or confront her. His fingers tapped at the paper. She flipped some more pages. Tucked some of her tawny hair behind her ear, a delicate tattoo of a wishing flower peeking out before the strands hid it again.

He wondered if it meant something or if it was just one of those cute, spur-of-the-moment designs she picked with her friends. He blinked the thought away— her style choices were none of his business, even if he was curious as an aspiring artist.

When she still didn't look up after Jericho had stood there for an ample amount of time, he started to get annoyed and cleared his throat obnoxiously. She started; her amber eyes were wide as one hand flew to cover her heart. When she realized who stood in front of her, she sighed.

"Do you need something?"

He held the paper out to her.

"Lena– one of my fellow art majors– said you were open to creativity."

He gestured to the paper now in her hands.

"I thought this would be an interesting take on the play while still keeping it semi-traditional."

She looked down at the design, blinking, but her face was otherwise unreadable. That is until she looked back up at Jericho.

She took her glasses off and tapped them against the paper.

"Are you trying to kiss my ass, Byers? Or were my drawings and swatches just not up to your standard?"

He balked.

"Excuse me?"

"I'm just having a hard time pinpointing your motive since you were an hour late. If you didn't care to be here in the first place, why would you put in any effort at all. Unless you want to get on my good side, or something?"

She placed a hand on her hip, her eyes blazing.

"Nice try. I'm not taking back your 'tardy' mark."

He almost rolled his eyes, but he kept his face carefully neutral. He knew it would do no good to explain to her that he had forgotten to set his alarm. And it would definitely not do to explain that he got home late the night before after working at a tattoo shop.

"Look, I'm sorry I was late, but you don't have to be such a hardass. I was just trying to contribute," he ground out.

She nodded her head and then shook it, letting out a humorless laugh, "Wow, that is *truly* an endearing apology. Does that work on all your professors?"

This time, Jericho did roll his eyes.

"Sometimes. Does being a type-A teacher's pet work better?"

She snapped her binder closed.

"Why don't you go do your part, since you have some catching up to do."

"Whatever you say, *professor*."

He scowled, turning on his heel.

Geeze, what's her deal?

Lena was obviously biting back a grin when Jericho sat down. Propping her chin on her hand she tilted her head.

"So, how'd it go?"

He pulled out the sketch from the director's pile that he thought looked the dumbest and handed it to his classmate.

"Peachy. We are doing this one."

She took the paper and made a face.

"This one?"

"Yup," he snapped.

Lena raised a brow.

"Okay, grumpy pants."

Jericho only grunted in return. He wasn't an extrovert by

any means, and making friends had never come naturally to him, but he had never met a person as aggravating as this director. He couldn't wait to get out of there to get some pizza and a few rounds of beer.

The rest of the class was uneventful. He assigned groups to work on different parts of the set and tucked the color swatch in his pocket so he could use it as a reference when he raided the art closet later for anything they could use.

At the end of the class, the director called them into the auditorium's center to check off her list. Jericho listened begrudgingly, and she seemed to avoid looking in his direction at all, even when addressing the art students he was in charge of.

He grabbed his bag and left as soon as it was over. He headed home to shower. And he hoped that he could wash off the irritation of those blazing amber eyes and smart mouth that lingered like an itch on his skin.

CHAPTER THREE

Marlee

She was halfway back to the dorm when her phone went off. She ignored it, wanting nothing but to go cozy up with a book after the day she had. Not that it was all bad.

After all, she was still directing one of her favorite stories. Not to mention she felt that they had already made some progress with the script. But the memory of Jericho's sarcastic remarks made her roll her eyes.

However, Marlee was determined not to let him ruin this for her. Her phone went off again. Then again. She stepped into the elevator and pressed the button for her floor. When her phone sounded yet again, she sighed and started to dig through the black hole that was her book bag.

"Ugghhhh–" she groaned, dropping pencils and other paraphernalia on the floor in her search.

Lost in the hunt for her illusive device, Marlee didn't register that the elevator doors had opened. When she finally found her phone, she looked up and blew the hair from her face. She blinked.

Ada, who had been texting her friend on her way down the hall, stood in front of the open doors. An amused smile tilted her lips.

"Dude, there you are," she laughed with a shake of her head. "I thought you were gonna blow us off."

Marlee glanced at the messages and then back at her friend. "What?"

The doors started to close and as she lurched forward to

stop them, Ada propped her foot in front of one instead.

She frowned, "Uh, Pizzarini?"

"Oh—"

Marlee blinked.

"C'mon, we are gonna be late. And I know how much you hate being late."

Her friend took one of her bags, ushering her down the hall.

"Ada, Pizzarini isn't in our dorm," Marlee laughed, a little confused why they were headed there instead.

Ada unlocked the door and pushed her friend inside.

"Girl, you look like a tornado hit."

"Huh?"

She looked down at her jeans and the baggy sweatshirt she wore, adjusting her glasses.

"I *mean,* put your books down, change your clothes and tame those tangles. Take a second to breathe, Mar."

She proceeded to help her put down all the things she was carrying and grabbed her hands.

"Okay, breathe with me—"

Marlee smiled, her hands coming up to hold onto her friend's elbows.

"Okay zen master, we don't have time for this. As you said, we are gonna be late. I'll go change and we can go."

After a quick hug, Marlee turned toward her room, calling out over her shoulder as she walked away, "Are we taking your car or mine?"

"Sanny is picking us up!"

Marlee rifled through her meager closet, and yelled back, "Sanjay's car is working again?"

Holding up a few different shirts she glanced at the selection of pants. She just wanted to be comfortable after the day she had. Deciding on a soft, knit sweater and leggings, she quickly changed.

"I guess we will find out! You know how unreliable that piece of junk is."

"Don't let him hear you say that!" Marlee laughed as she threw her hair up into a messy bun and then grabbed her purse.

She glanced out the window, spotting their friend sitting

on the hood of his mustard-colored beater car. Marlee had no idea what make or model it was, she just knew it was so ugly that it was kind of cute. Coming out into the living space she held out her arms, seeking Ada's approval of her transformation.

"Beautiful, *darling*," Ada grinned, winking a gray-blue eye.

"Thanks."

Marlee motioned in the general direction of the parking lot.

"He's here."

Ada shook her phone as she headed out the door, "I know, he's asking if he needs to get his affairs in order. Apparently, we are taking so long that he's afraid he will die of old age."

"What a drama queen," Marlee snorted.

"Let's go. Can't keep gramps waiting too long."

It didn't take them long to get down to the car. Since most students were out and about after class, it left the halls of the dorm and the plaza pretty empty. Sanjay hopped off the hood of his car upon seeing the girls, a wide grin pulling out his dimples.

"Finally! I thought I'd never see you two again."

"Sorry, Mar was having a crisis."

Marlee rolled her eyes at Ada.

"I was not."

"You didn't have your sugary magic bean juice this morning—of course, you were having a crisis," Sanjay snickered.

She crossed her arms.

"If only I had a friend who knew my coffee order and walked it over to me from the cart."

"I guess you are gonna have to make some more friends," Sanjay sighed heavily.

"Rude."

They laughed and piled into his car.

Ada beat Marlee to shotgun and immediately turned the radio on full blast. Riding with Sanjay and Ada was always enjoyable, so she felt right at home when they were belting the lyrics to Justin Bieber's 'Baby' with the windows down so every passerby could hear them.

They stared at the empty, rounded booth that their group

frequented. Their friend, August, was normally the first to get there. He was usually the one to order the pizza and somehow ensured everyone got their favorites.

Ada frowned, pulling out her phone.

Marlee looked back at the door.

"August isn't here yet?"

"He's always talking to people, maybe he got held up." Sanjay shrugged and slid into the booth, eyeing Ada as she started texting.

"Yeah," she said distractedly.

Marlee slid into the other side of the booth and grabbed a menu.

"Well, I'm starving. Maybe we should order a pizza while we wait?"

When neither of her friends answered, she looked up at Ada, who was still distracted as her fingers flew over the keyboard. Then she glanced at Sanjay. His face was unreadable as he stared blankly at the table, tugging on one of his raven-colored curls. Reaching across, she tapped her fingers where he was staring.

He blinked.

She tilted her head.

"You okay?"

"Oh, yeah, sorry, just tired," he told her and smiled as he patted her fingers back.

The corner of her mouth lifted softly.

"Okay."

Ada slid her phone into the back pocket of her jeans and adjusted the edge of her crop tee. "Yeah, he's almost here. Apparently, he had a friend to pick up."

"Should we wait to order then?" Marlee asked.

Sanjay's eyebrows rose, suddenly interested.

"A friend?"

Ada nodded and sat beside him, smiling as she fluffed his curls.

"You look nice today, Sanny. Your hair is getting so long."

He gently swatted her hand away, laughing, "Thanks."

Marlee watched as Ada returned to her phone when it went

off again and Sanjay ducked his blushing face away.

What the heck is that all about?

Before she could think any more about that, the doors to Pizzarini opened. A bellowing laugh floated and echoed around the room. It could only belong to August.

Ada stood up, waving at him. Marlee turned to do the same but froze when she caught sight of an all-too-familiar moth tattoo.

Oh hell no.

CHAPTER FOUR

Jericho

Jericho followed August through the array of tables, still blissfully ignorant of the coming storm. It wasn't until they were a few feet from the booth that his friend moved out of his line of view, and he finally made eye contact with the director.

His jaw tightened.

August clapped a large hand on Jericho's shoulder, grinning so widely that his eyes almost crinkled shut.

"Sorry I'm late, guys. I had to pick up this guy."

Jericho gave a tentative smile. He wished his gaze would stop bumping into hers.

"Uh, Jericho, this is Ada," he said, motioning to the girl with wild blonde curls.

"Hey!" She smiled, lifting her hand in a small wave. Jericho lifted his chin in greeting.

"That's Sanjay."

August fist-bumped the guy.

Jericho smiled a little, "Hi."

His friend moved on to the director and Jericho tried his best to keep his facial expression unaffected.

"And this is Marlee, one of my oldest friends."

"We've met, actually," she said, bending the laminated menu back and forth.

Jericho crossed his arms as he mumbled, "'Met' is one way to put it."

August's hazel eyes flicked between the two. Marlee's cheeks turned pink. She cleared her throat and stood abruptly.

"Let's go order that pizza, August."

The man didn't even get to answer as Marlee grabbed hold of his sleeve and dragged him away.

Jericho smiled awkwardly at the other two. Sanjay's downturned smile quickly faded as he motioned to the booth.

"Uh, sit wherever you want bro."

Ada nodded, moving to the other side where Marlee had vacated her seat.

"Yeah, I'll just move and sit next to Mar," she commented, though her eyes wandered toward the front of the restaurant after her friends.

"Thanks."

It seemed he had no choice but to endure this get-together. He didn't doubt that these people were fun or nice, but Marlee was clearly as uncomfortable as Jericho.

Social gatherings with strangers should be listed as torture.

"Damn, that tattoo is sick. Who did it?" Sanjay asked with wide eyes as he studied the moth inked on the front of Jericho's throat.

Jericho blinked as the question pulled him out of his thoughts.

"Oh– thanks. I actually drew the design and started the stencil. With my mentor's help, I completed all the finishing touches."

"Badass," Sanjay replied with an approving nod. He tilted his head.

"What kind of moth is it? I feel like I've seen it before."

"It's called something like... African death's-head hawkmoth, I think." Jericho shrugged with a half-smile.

He was starting to feel more comfortable, but he knew it would end as soon as the director— Marlee, got back to the table.

Sanjay grinned, adjusting his glasses.

"Ah yes. *Archerontia atropos.*" His dark skin reddened as he scratched his head. "Sorry, biology major here who loves bugs."

In truth, Jericho was impressed. It seemed to him that Sanjay was passionate about his major, and that was something he could understand.

"All good. Art major here who loves specific paint or variations of brushes and could name them all," he laughed.

Sanjay smiled back.

"So . . . how do you know Mar?" Ada asked as she set her phone down.

"I don't know her."

When she frowned, he waved a hand in the general direction of campus and added, "We just met today— working on the production for the end of term."

Sanjay rubbed a hand over his smile. Ada nodded as she laughed, "Ah. So, you've seen her in 'Evil Stepmother' mode."

The corner of Jericho's mouth twitched. It seemed Marlee's friends were familiar with the woman he had encountered today. And even though she had irritated the shit out of him, he knew that people were paintings with many colors.

"Is she usually like that?"

"Just when she's late."

"Or when she forgets her coffee," Sanjay added.

Ada grinned.

"Or when someone chews too loud."

"Or when she feels itchy."

"When she loses in a video game."

"Oh! And remember that time she was pissed for a week because you rearranged our cupboard, Sanjay?"

He shook his head, a broad smile on his face.

"She even turned her nose up at the cookies I had made."

Jericho blinked.

It sounded like they were poking fun at Marlee with fondness. But it didn't stop him from wondering how they put up with her. He wasn't sure how he would handle that for the rest of the term. Especially if she turned "Evil Stepmother" at any small thing he'd say or do.

Let's hope there's some Cinderella in there too.

"To be fair, you messed up her system," Ada laughed.

Sanjay held up his hands. "Okay, but I made her cookies?"

"But you gave her cookies on a Tuesday, Sanny."

"Oh, right."

Jericho frowned. "What are you guys talking about?"

"No sweets on Tuesdays," Ada droned.

Sanjay nodded emphatically.

"No exceptions."

"Why?"

"Because Monday is gelato day." Sanjay shrugged.

"Every Monday?"

Ada grinned, "Yeah, it's mandatory."

Jericho shook his head, muttering under his breath, "What a hot mess."

And that was the moment *she* returned.

He pressed his back into the booth, bracing for her reaction because he was sure that she had heard him. But she didn't even spare him a glance. He wasn't sure whether that was a good or bad sign.

August didn't even ask him to scoot as he bumped into Jericho, pushing him further into the booth. Jericho gave him a sidelong glance.

Fuck you.

"Where's the parm packets, Auggie?" Ada slapped the table, her voice suddenly deeper than Sanjay's.

August turned his hat around, pulling two packets from his pocket before tossing them across the table.

"Bro, I got you."

Ada's nose scrunched in the middle, batting the packets away.

"Ew, what are those, three months old?"

"I grabbed them from the front a few minutes ago!" He laughed as he looked at Marlee, "Back me up here."

"Huh?"

"Tell the woman I don't hoard cheese in my gym shorts."

Loosely turning to Ada, she repeated, "He doesn't hoard

cheese in his gym shorts."

Sanjay picked up the parmesan packets and stacked them in the center of the table. "By the power vested in me by ... by the Lord of the Beans ... I proclaim these packets full of BS!"

Jericho watched as the table laughed. Sanjay's eyes were bound to Ada. But Ada's were focused on August. And August's were closed entirely by laughter.

Well, that's awkward.

Marlee was grinning but Jericho could tell she was trying in vain not to be grumpy.

Her eyebrows are a dead giveaway.

He watched as her fingers drummed on the table, and before he knew it, his feet joined in the rhythm. Realizing this he pushed his soles flat on the ground.

Let's not overthink that.

"Where's the 'za?" Ada asked.

"Probably not gonna be here for a century since he-man over here ordered seven of them." Marlee rested her chin on her fist, her eyes flicking to August.

All of them are staring at him. Typical.

"Seven isn't an unreasonable amount of pizza!" He argued.

"Seven *extra-large,* stuffed crust pizzas with extra cheese and toppings?"

"A man's gotta eat, Mar!"

His large hand slapped the table.

"You know what, I don't have to defend myself to you. You used to be fun, you know? Remember the eating contest of '09? You wiped the floor with everyone. Or, more accurately, the table."

Marlee's face turned red.

Ada covered her mouth with her hand as her eyebrows raised.

"And I'm just hearing about this now?" Sanjay laughed.

August opened his mouth to relay the tale, but Marlee spoke first, "It's irrelevant."

"It's embarrassing, you mean?" She said with a laugh.

Almost like she was teasing.

Almost.

"I wanna know how many burgers you annihilated!"

Marlee glanced over her shoulder again, spotting the approaching waiters who were bringing the pizza.

"Oh look, here comes the pizza!"

"Hell yeah, grubs up!" August boomed, making Jericho jump.

Damn, I'm getting whiplash with this group.

He thought hanging with August was a lot some days, but he felt a little like he needed a nap after this. Thankfully as the pizza was set out there was much less talking.

But as her friends began to reach for the various slices, Marlee went on slapping hands away.

"Dude!" Sanjay laughed.

Jericho watched as she began to cut the slices herself and after Sanjay's reaction, nobody said another word about it.

Marlee set a slice of pizza on Jericho's plate, her amber eyes bright as her eyebrow lifted. "Wouldn't want to make a *hot mess*."

CHAPTER FIVE

Marlee

The remaining days of the weekend were very much needed for Marlee after the tension at Pizzarini. She hadn't expected to have to interact with Jericho outside of the theater, and every time she thought about how the conversation had gone down, the more embarrassed she got.

But it didn't matter— not really. She didn't need him to like her.

Right?

Shaking herself out of her thoughts, she pushed through the doors to the auditorium— this time with coffee in hand. She had learned her lesson that first day. This time she was prepared. With a more professional-looking outfit, her tawny layers tied up into a long, sleek ponytail, her makeup actually done, and complete with updated notes in her binder.

Taking off her coat and setting her things down in one of the chairs, she took a deep breath and looked around the empty auditorium.

At least I beat everyone here this time.

The sound of a door opening made her turn. She perked up, thinking that, maybe, the others had decided to be more serious about the production. Seeing Jericho come through the doors instead, she blinked.

He was the last person she had expected to be on time, let alone early. He paused, his gaze sweeping over the empty room and settling on her. They exchanged an awkward, tense smile before Marlee returned to her binder.

After the doors shut, she had hoped that he would go to start setting up for the set crew. But he approached her instead. Her pulse quickened. Irritation and embarrassment mingled in her chest, heating her cheekbones. She didn't dare look at him, pretending to read her notes in her binder.

Until he cleared his throat.

Looking up, one of her brows twitched, and despite trying to keep her mouth shut, she lost the battle.

"Splurge on an alarm clock this weekend?"

She saw the flash of annoyance under his stony exterior, and for some reason that made her want to smile.

He dropped a hand into the pocket of his ripped jeans and looked at his feet for a moment.

"Look, we obviously got off on the wrong foot the other day. . ."

She didn't comment to agree with him, even though she did, and her silence spurred him on.

"I just wanted to say, I won't be late again."

Marlee closed her binder and nodded. "I will hold you to that."

He nodded back.

"Alright—" Pointing toward the other side of the auditorium he took a step backward.

"I should go set up for the crew to do some work."

"Yeah," she replied lamely and then he left to do as he had said. She really hadn't expected that.

Glancing at the clock she figured that she had about five minutes before her cast showed up.

Hopefully.

With her binder under her arm and her coffee in her hand, she moved up to the stage and took a seat on the edge. Then she began adding notes about music selections in the margin of her papers, taking sips of coffee here and there.

Tapping the end of her pen on the paper she glanced over at where Jericho was setting up a portable table.

Do all of his t-shirts have paint on them?

Setting her coffee down, Marlee leaned back on her hands, watching as he set the table legs. His biceps flexed as his hand smacked the locks in place.

This makes me feel nothing.

He set down what she guessed to be a sketchbook on the table and leaned over it. A dark lock of his hair tumbled over his forehead.

Okay, so he's attractive, so what? He's still lazy and a jerk, she told herself.

When he brushed the hair away from his face, she noticed just how dark and long his eyelashes were. Realizing she had started to chew on the end of her pen, she shook her head.

Ugh.

"Hey, Marlee."

Ripping her gaze from Jericho, she finally noticed that a group of the cast had shown up. Moving the binder off her lap and hopping down from the stage she rubbed her palms over the wrinkles forming on the front of her black slacks.

"Hi, guys!" She greeted, ignoring the warm burning on her cheekbones.

Bennet held up his script.

"Are we running lines this morning?"

"Yes. I would really like everyone to have the first half of their lines memorized as soon as possible," she answered loudly for the group.

"Preferably by the end of this week? Is that doable?" She gave Bennet a hopeful look.

"Let's just make it the goal."

Not wholly the answer she was looking for, but it was something. With a nod, Marlee looked over the crowd of actors.

"Where's my Belle?"

A girl with whom Marlee shared a videography class came forward.

"Belle here. AKA— Talia. Hey." Talia smiled and so did Marlee.

The rest of the session went smoothly. Talia and Bennet had been cast by Mr. Emery, so before meeting them, Marlee had been a bit apprehensive. Having leads that were either too lazy or incompetent was her worst nightmare.

Thankfully, the two were neither of these things.

And they proved that as the day went on. The cast ran lines and helped each other rehearsing. The piano was being used to find the correct starting pitch for the songs. And the set design crew even seemed to be working.

As the cast left, some said goodbye or waved, and others slipped out of the auditorium quietly. Marlee breathed a sigh of relief that she had gotten through the day without any hiccups.

Glancing toward the set crew, who had also started to leave, she squared her shoulders. She needed to touch base with Jericho about the set. Earlier, she had found his original design lodged in her binder. And a second look made her realize that she had been too quick to dismiss the idea.

The color scheme was nice to look at and the sketches... well they weren't bad.

Marlee had a hard time admitting that she liked any ideas other than her own. But if she wanted to go anywhere in the theater world, she would need to be able to work well with others.

So, she would try.

Dumping the empty coffee cup into the trash, she tucked her binder under her arm and approached Jericho. Pausing a few feet from the table where he was talking to Lena, she waited for her to leave. She tried not to listen or watch the conversation between the two, but it was odd to see Jericho making expressive facial expressions.

Even stranger was the fact that the girl refused to leave. They both seemed to enjoy each other's company.

Where they friends? Or more? she wondered.

"You did not just say that!" Lena laughed.

At something Jericho said? Since when was he funny?

His returning smile made Marlee twitch a little. Feeling

slightly out of place, she shifted on her feet. Nevertheless, she moved closer hoping Lena would notice and take her leave.

Unfortunately, Jericho noticed first.

"Do you need something?"

He was still smiling as he said it. That somehow made it so much worse for Marlee.

"I—" Her gaze shifted briefly to Lena who was now also staring at her.

"I was hoping to touch base about the set."

"What about it?" asked Lena as if she had every intention of participating.

Marlee adjusted her binder under her arm.

"I had some questions about Jericho's design."

She thought that Lena would take the veiled hint that this was a question for Jericho, but the girl stayed rooted like a tree.

Or like August at a sushi bar.

"The design you rejected without looking at?"

She didn't know if Lena was coming after her for insulting Jericho or if she were simply teasing. Either way, she was slightly impressed by her for saying it.

Jericho's eyes widened at his friend's boldness.

Marlee's face heated as she pulled out the design.

"Well, I've looked at it *now*."

Jericho's eyebrow twitched up just a little.

"And what did you think?" He crossed his arms.

"It's a... nice idea," Marlee started slowly.

It looked like Jericho was trying not to smirk. "It needs work— but it is a good place to start."

"Well, shit, let's get started!"

Since the hints had gone over Lena's head, Marlee turned her burning amber eyes on her. It seemed to do the trick.

"Oh, you know what? I just remembered I have somewhere to be—" Lena blinked and picked up her things, motioning to the doors.

Jericho and Marlee watched her leave even after the doors closed.

Jericho ran a hand through his hair, avoiding her eyes. Marlee did the same for a moment. The comment about her being a 'hot mess' kept replaying in her head right after the bit about being a 'type-A teacher's pet' and she hated that those words were enough to make her feel small.

Gathering her courage, she looked up, their gazes colliding.

"You had questions?" he asked.

She nodded, setting the design down on the table.

"Yeah, um—" Pointing to the sketch of the beast's costume, she frowned. "Why does the Beast look like a boar?"

"It's the original design."

"Uh, I've seen the original movie probably a thousand times. He does not look like that."

"Not the movie. The book."

Marlee blinked.

Jericho's brows lifted.

"*La Belle et la Bête*?"

He... He reads?

"Oh, right," she responded robotically.

This makes me feel nothing.

Turning her attention back to the design, she nodded. "So, you want to do a fusion of the book and the movie?"

"Yeah, I thought it would be a good challenge. And maybe appeal to a wider audience," he explained as he leaned on the table next to her.

His finger pointed at the concept for Belle's dress.

"Sasha is obsessed with period fashion and would jump at the chance to do something like this."

"Cool. I'll have to check with Mr. Emery about the budget for that."

"Okay."

After a pause, he straightened, crossing his arms again.

"So, anything else?"

"I have notes on the color scheme, but we can go over that another time." Tucking the design back into the binder Marlee tried to smile. He nodded.

"Okay, well, cool."

"Cool cool cool," he echoed.

Her hand waved awkwardly as she muttered goodbye and left. As soon as she exited the building she leaned heavily against the door— her breath suddenly becoming heavy.

What the fuck...

CHAPTER SIX

Jericho

When Jericho returned to the dorm August was gone. Which was a regular occurrence. Funnily enough, he counted himself lucky to land a roommate who was so extroverted that he was either gone with friends or spending the night elsewhere most of the time.

So more often than not, Jericho had the dorm to himself. Not that he had never come home to a bunch of frat boys and a keg before, but after one particular incident, it seemed that August was more mindful of Jericho's space.

Which was why Jericho considered him a friend.

Dumping his backpack on the threadbare couch he decided to grill a sandwich, taking his time and enjoying the solitude. Most of all, he was just glad to get away from everyone asking him so many questions.

He slapped the bread butter side down in the hot pan and layered some cheese on top. Opening the fridge, he realized he had forgotten to stop at the store on his way back. All they had was some cheese and wilted vegetables. He opened the cupboard and rolled his eyes, half smiling.

And a shit ton of spam. Of course.

He cooked more than his roommate but when August made spam and eggs in the morning it wasn't horrible.

Taking a can out Jericho peeled the top off and added two thin slices on top of the melting cheese, then covered it with the other piece of bread. Standing there, occasionally bumping the sandwich around, his mind was still racing. And as much as he wanted to zone out and empty his head after the day, he couldn't.

That last conversation with *her* had caught him off guard. He kept replaying things she had said and analyzing the tiniest details of the conversation. He thought about his responses and how he might have worded things better.

The near-constant blush on Marlee's cheeks had been distracting him as well— trying to figure it out. She didn't strike him as the nervous type.

She was probably just annoyed that she actually liked my idea.

He half-smiled.

But it faded quickly.

It probably had nothing to do with him. She could have just been overheated.

Obviously. This is just me overthinking. I am the furthest thing from her mind.

The aggressive sizzling from the pan jolted him out of those thoughts. Cursing under his breath, Jericho picked up the spatula and hurried to flip the sandwich. Now burnt black from his lack of attention.

That's not ominous at all.

Jericho made sure to set his alarm early every night before the theater classes. And while the tension seemed to ease up when he was on time, it didn't stop the heated discussions from happening. Especially when Marlee had seen a very rough version of Lumiere's costume.

Apparently using real fire was 'too much, even for her'.

Even though I made sure it was perfectly safe.

He was keeping himself so busy with the set preparations and his internship that most nights he almost passed out while trying to eat his dinner or do homework.

And, today, it finally caught up with him. Because here he was, almost five minutes late.

Jericho didn't think he had ever run to class before, and the fact that he had been doing all of this to appease *her* irritated the hell out of him. He didn't know why he kept doing it.

Why do I even care? She's not my teacher.

Coming in the doors, he tried to catch his breath— hoping no one would notice that he looked, smelled, and sounded like he had just run miles to get here and not only across the campus. The two leads, Bennet and Talia, were already inside at their usual spot with a few of the others. Marlee was talking to Lena.

Shit.

Jericho shrugged out of his jacket, using it to wipe the beading sweat at his hairline as his eyes darted between the director and his friend. He hoped that maybe she wouldn't see him.

And for a moment he thought he had pulled it off.

He convinced himself that five minutes wasn't a big deal, but as he passed by, Marlee's eyes immediately found him, and the blazing amber was enough for him to know. It was indeed a big deal.

He paused, holding her gaze as he set his sketchbook down on the table. But she turned back to Lena instead.

Cold shoulder. So mature.

He rolled his eyes and decided to immerse himself in his work. She could do enough fretting for the both of them.

Avoidance seemed to work in his favor up until people were leaving. And like an approaching storm, he could almost imagine the room darkening and even the thunder roaring as she approached.

"You were late."

"What, no 'hello'?" he droned.

"I told you I would hold you to it."

He tried not to sigh.

I am too tired for this.

"To what?"

"Your word," she snapped.

"You said you wouldn't be late again. And yet..." She gestured with her arm.

"It's five minutes, Marlee."

"Time is valuable. Especially here. Every minute counts toward the resulting production. If we are lazy, the scou— crowd will know!"

He stared at her. She stared back, crossing her arms as if she hadn't just revealed her hand.

So that's why she's so wound up.

Rubbing a hand over his face he decided to leave that alone and changed the subject.

"We still haven't gone over color schemes for the backdrops. We're gonna need to know them for the mock-ups."

She looked at her watch.

"I have a class in about an hour and fifteen. We could go look now?"

He wanted to object and just go back to his dorm to nap. Or paint. He hadn't had time to paint anything original lately and it was starting to get to him. But the expectant lift of her brows told him he better not, so he conceded.

"Sure."

They didn't speak as they walked across campus to the art building. He was thankful for the stretch of silence. It was oddly comfortable considering their earlier argument. But he tried not to think about that.

Jericho walked ahead of her into the classroom, his eyes glancing at the closet before shuffling the keys in his hand. He ignored the feeling of Marlee's stare.

"So, what are your concerns about the color scheme?" he asked as he fit the correct key in the lock.

"I actually don't have any concerns. Just a few suggestions."

He glanced at her as she sipped her coffee.

"Suggestions?"

She nodded, giving him a funny look.

He bit back a laugh.

"Why are you laughing?"

Turning the lock, he shook his head and lied, "I'm not."

"If you have something to say, by all means, say it," she challenged.

Opening the door, he looked at her, weighing his options.

She tapped her foot and tilted her head, sending her tawny curls rippling over her shoulder like a gentle waterfall.

His jaw twitched.

"Your suggestions are more like demands."

It had taken most of his energy to voice the reply. Needless to say, her stunned silence was exactly the effect he had hoped for. But as he opened the door, she regained her voice and Jericho started looking through the supply closet for the colors they wanted to try out.

"I'm responsible for this production. I have to make demands, or nothing will get done. We would all be stuck at the drawing board if—"

"Hold the door, it locks from the outside," Jericho interrupted as he handed her the keys.

Going back to the closet, he set aside small jars so they could test them on a sketch first. But he only had one hand as he held the door open with the other and glanced at Marlee who was still talking.

"Everyone is always complaining—"

He interrupted again, "Can you hold the door?"

The way her eyes lit up with frustration and how she opened her mouth to speak again, he should have known that she wasn't really listening to him.

Too focused on defending herself, she continued, "I have been very open to ideas and creative vision so far."

"Uh-huh," he muttered, letting go of the door.

As it started to swing shut Marlee squeaked, "Wait–!"

She hopped inside instead of catching the door, her coffee cup colliding with Jericho's chest as he turned.

"Shit!"

"My coffee!"

The door slammed shut behind her.

They stared at the splatter on his shirt's front and then the empty cup where it rolled across the floor. Jericho's fight or flight kicked in as he realized what had just happened. Reaching around her his hand found the doorknob and he wrestled with it frantically.

No.

His eyes darted to her other hand that still clutched the keys.

She followed his gaze to her hand, opening her fingers. With a nervous laugh, she held them up.

"At least we have the keys?"

"It locks from the outside," Jericho growled.

Her face paled.

"Oh—"

"I asked you to hold the door."

"My hands were full!"

"Use your back! Or your elbow— or something!"

They glared at each other.

Marlee's cheeks turned color.

Jericho's neck heated.

She broke eye contact first, reaching behind herself to pull out her phone.

"I'll see if August can get us out of here," she said, pressing call. Her phone and the backs of her fingers bumped against his chest.

Jericho's jaw twitched.

This closet is too damn small for both of us.

Jericho tried to back up and put space between them, but he bumped into the shelves. Marlee tried to call August again.

Being sent to voicemail for a second time, she chewed her lip.

"He's probably in class. What time is it?" Before he could answer she looked for herself. "3:11— yeah, he won't be out of his biochemistry class for another forty minutes. I'll try Sanjay."

Jericho bumped his head against a shelf, rubbing his hand over his face.

"Even if they answer, they need keys."

Marlee slowly dropped the phone away from her ear and hung up when Sanjay didn't answer either.

"August knows Ms. Roland and could probably get her over here to unlock the door. Or I could call Lena. She also has a set of keys."

"Okay."

While Jericho called Lena, Marlee texted August in hopes that someone would come to save them from the torture of proximity.

CHAPTER SEVEN

Marlee

It had been painfully awkward silence for the last fifteen minutes. Lena hadn't picked up her phone, and August still hadn't texted back. Jericho looked like he would crawl right under the door if it were possible.

Marlee felt much the same. There was barely an inch between them and every time he moved they were accidentally touching.

Looking at the coffee stain again she bit her lips together. Marlee knew that there were many other reasons why she was irritated. And, admittedly, many of them didn't have anything to do with Jericho.

But somehow, she found herself taking it out on him.

Lifting her eyes as much as she dared, she studied the tiny details of the moth tattoo on his neck. Every line was clean, and the shading truly was impressive.

It's beautiful.

Her gaze moved past the firm lines of his jaw and finally met his eyes. The two had been casually ignoring each other, but it was impossible to pretend any longer for Marlee.

So, she swallowed her pride.

"Sorry," she apologized.

He studied her and then looked away.

"It will wash out."

She had meant to apologize for her attitude, but he must have seen her looking at the coffee stain and assumed.

About to clarify, she barely opened her mouth when Jericho added, "I think there are some shirts in here we use for protection during class. . ."

Marlee frowned.

"Huh?"

But Jericho didn't offer any explanation as he lifted his arms toward a box on one of the shelves. As his armpit hovered in her face, she tried to back up and accidentally elbowed him in the ribcage.

"Ow," he groused, almost dropping the box on their heads.

Marlee glared at him, resisting the urge to slap him away. The fact that she wasn't put off by the aroma was actually off-putting.

"Dude— get your smelly pits out of my face."

"Whose fault is it that we are in this damn closet, again?" He shot back as he lowered the box enough to pull a random shirt out and then shoved it back onto the shelf.

Marlee started to speak but with the way Jericho's arm came down, the fabric slapped over her face. Blowing out a puff of air to get the hair out of her face she placed her hands on her hips.

"You didn't warn me you were closing the door or that it locked from the outside!"

"I did. You just weren't listening."

"When?"

"When I gave you the keys!"

She blinked.

At the moment, she truly hadn't registered what he had said to her when he handed her the keys. But the more she thought about it, and the succession of events that had followed, she realized that she really hadn't been listening.

Tucking her hair behind her ears she let out a breath.

"I don't know why I didn't hear you say that," she said quietly.

That's a lie.

"Because you were busy talking," he replied flatly.

She had to bite down on the inside of her cheek to stop herself from arguing.

Why do I feel the need to oppose everything he says or does?

"I. . ." Marlee struggled with herself.

She needed to apologize because her stress was getting the better of her, but it was slightly embarrassing for her to admit this.

"I'm sorry for not listening."

He stared at her, the tiniest crease forming between his brows.

Her face started to feel hot again as she added, "I shouldn't take my stress out on you."

She couldn't tell what he thought about her apology. Marlee didn't think that she could blame him for being hesitant to accept her words.

Jericho started to lift the bottom of his shirt, a half-smile tilting his lips, "Don't sweat it."

With a roll of her eyes, Marlee laughed lightly, "Just take the apology."

She saw a flash of a smirk before he pulled his shirt over his head.

"Is that a demand or a suggestion?"

She couldn't help the easy smile that played over her lips.

"Ha. Ha."

As he rolled the soiled shirt in on itself, she couldn't help how her eyes were drawn to the other tattoos on his skin.

A line of cursive writing ran along his ribs. A symbol she didn't recognize on the front of his shoulder. And something on his hipbone that was half hidden by the band of his pants.

Quickly blinking away from the sight of him, she made the mistake of looking up and their gazes collided again. Turning to the shelves she studied the jars of paint and other supplies like they were masterpieces in a gallery.

Stop blushing. Stop blushing. Stop—

"Do you want a new shirt?"

She looked at him.

"What? I have a shirt."

I'm an idiot.

"I—I know. I meant a *new* one."

Is he blushing?

She shook her head. "I'm okay."

"You have coffee all over you."

"It's not that bad."

Marlee looked down at her shirt.

It's worse.

"I can grab another one—"

"I'm not changing in front of you!"

"I was going to turn around!"

He raked a hand through his hair.

He's definitely blushing.

"No."

She crossed her arms.

"Please don't do that."

He pinched the bridge of his nose.

"Do what?"

"Stubborn..." he mumbled to himself and reached up to the box again.

This time he grabbed two shirts. He dropped one in her hands and held up the other with a raise of his brows, proceeding to blindfold himself.

Marlee scrunched the fabric in her fingers and relented. The shirt *was* uncomfortable and sticky. And he was being very nice. She didn't think he was the type of guy to peek, anyways.

Hurrying to take her shirt off, she had just set it down on the shelf and held the other in her hands when the lock clicked. She froze when she should have just put the damn shirt on.

She half-turned, holding the other shirt over her chest. Lena looked like she was just as shocked as Marlee to find the director and lead set designer like this.

Thankfully, Marlee was able to refrain from spewing the age-old deflection, 'It's not what it looks like!'.

Though, she wasn't sure if silence was any better.

"Oh. Am I interrupting—?"

"NO!" Both Jericho and Marlee practically shouted in unison.

Lena's smile grew though she was visibly trying not to laugh as she covered her mouth and nodded. Marlee quickly yanked the shirt over her head. Jericho ripped off the blindfold.

"Hey, no judgment here, it can get boring being locked in a closet, gotta find ways to pass the time," Lena joked, not even able to get through the first half of her sentence without giggling.

Jericho looked like Marlee felt.

Like I wanna flush myself down the nearest toilet.

"Shut up," she muttered, red-faced.

"And if you breathe a word of this mishap to anyone, your ass is grass," she barked and stomped out of the room.

◆ ◆ ◆

It had been a couple of days since *the incident*, and Marlee had mostly recovered. So far, Lena hadn't brought it up to her or anyone else that she knew of. Which she was thankful for.

Though, there was a sort of laughing light in her eyes whenever Marlee spoke to her.

Checking the last box on her list of things to accomplish during today's rehearsal, she sighed and closed her binder.

"Good job guys, see you at the next meeting. Remember to have the first act memorized by then, please," she addressed the group.

Bennet high-fived her on his way out. "See ya next time, Boss."

"See ya," she laughed.

The auditorium quieted as she began to gather her things, and all she could think about was going home and having her free hour to snuggle in some blankets and eat whatever leftover pizza they had from the other night.

With her things in hand, she turned to leave but paused upon seeing Jericho standing a few feet away.

"Need something?" Marlee asked, willing her cheeks not to turn red.

He looked down at the bundle in his hands and shook his head.

"Uh– no. I just thought you might want this back."

He held up what appeared to be a folded piece of clothing. Marlee frowned.

"Might want what back?"

She took a step toward him at the same time he came closer.

"You left it behind the other day . . ."

Oh.

He tilted his head as he handed her the shirt she had left behind in the closet. She took it.

"Oh. Right."

Marlee turned it over in her hands, smiling.

"Thank you."

"Don't sweat it," he teased, smiling back. She almost snorted. "See you, Marlee."

"Bye."

She waved, watching him walk away, and hugged her binder tightly to her fluttering chest. Looking closer at the shirt, she realized he had washed it. She lifted it to her nose and breathed in the clean-smelling detergent. She smiled to herself.

Maybe he isn't such a jerk.

CHAPTER EIGHT

Jericho

Each of August's large hands held onto Jericho and Sanjay's shoulders, steering them into the bar.

"Let's ask for outdoor seating so we can drink and putt-putt," he suggested.

Sanjay clapped his hands together. "Sounds good to me."

"Putt-putt?" Jericho half laughed.

"Mini golf, my dude."

August grinned, slapping Jericho's shoulder twice before talking to the hostess at the front.

"You've never played?" Sanjay asked with raised brows.

Jericho shrugged.

"Maybe when I was a kid. Just never heard it called 'putt-putt' before."

Sanjay smiled, his dimples pulling.

August waved the guys forward as the hostess led them to the outdoor seating. Sanjay glanced behind them and then around the area. He frowned.

"Where's our Betty and Veronica?"

August checked his phone.

"Late."

"Who?"

Sanjay sent Jericho a sheepish smile.

"Oh, Marlee and Ada— sorry that's what I call them sometimes."

"Oh."

Jericho thought that was oddly fitting. He glanced at his watch as well.

Oh damn, they are late.

"This is history in the making," Sanjay laughed.

August grinned. "We can't let it go unrewarded. Even though it's probably Ada's fault."

"What, Marlee's never been late in her entire life?" Jericho crossed his arms.

I wouldn't be surprised. But nobody is that perfect.

"Like this? Nah. Being on time is her late."

"Except that one time—"

"The great coffee famine of orientation week," August interrupted Sanjay.

Jericho half-smiled.

"Do you hear yourself when you talk?"

"What! It was a dark day in the history of Marlee Firth-Diaz."

"Firth-Diaz?" Jericho quietly muttered to himself.

Her last name, most likely.

Sanjay took off his jacket and hung it over one of the chairs.

"So, I'm guessing you have a plan to mark this momentous occasion, Auggie?"

August stood, taking a minute to re-tie his man bun of dreads further up on his head. He held up his hands.

"Okay, here's the game plan." He put his hands together and pointed at Jericho and Sanjay, then to himself in a sweeping motion. "We hide. Then, when Ada, Marlee, and Lena walk in and don't see us, you *know* that Mar will hit that speed dial to scold us, so we—"

"We jump out and turn the tables on them! Genius."

Sanjay acted like his mind had been blown, gesturing an explosion with his fingers.

"Hey, don't act so surprised. The brain is a muscle too. And I don't slack."

He proceeded to flex. Jericho shook his head, amused.

"Alright, Buffy Barnes, let's do this." Sanjay fist-bumped

August.

Even though Jericho laughed, he brushed a hand back and forth through the back of his hair.

"Yeah, I don't know you guys."

"C'mon, I know how much flak she's been giving you. You don't want just a *little* bit of revenge?" August snickered.

Jericho hesitated.

That wasn't untrue. But they had been on better terms lately and he didn't want to backtrack.

"I mean, he could stay out here so when she arrives the first thing, she sees is that 'Lazy Jerry' beat her here. Now that would fry her noodle."

Sanjay and August laughed together. Jericho's brows rose, almost laughing himself.

Whatever that means...

And then the nickname registered.

He held up his hand. "Wait— 'Lazy Jerry'?"

But he didn't get an answer as August started shoving and slapping at his and Sanjay's backs.

"Shhh! They're here! Hide!"

In a mad dash, Jericho had no choice but to be hauled behind a half wall that separated the outdoor seating from the mini golf register. And so, he was sandwiched between Sanjay and August who both almost couldn't stop giggling like a pair of tween boys who had just played an epic prank on the girls they were too afraid to talk to.

Hearing the girls come into the outdoor seating area, the boys quieted.

"Okay, we made it, and before you guys say—" Marlee started, but cut off abruptly upon seeing the empty seating area. "Where are they?"

"I told you not to worry," Ada laughed.

Jericho heard Marlee sigh as she pulled out her phone.

"What are you doing?"

"Calling Sanny to see where the hell they are," Marlee

answered.

August shared a loaded look with Sanjay as he pulled out his phone. He answered on the first ring.

"Hey!" He said in a voice that was a little too high-pitched. "Where are you?"

And that was when August and Sanjay stepped out.

"Well, look who decided to show up?" August grinned.

Sanjay grabbed Jericho's shoulder, bringing him closer to the two boys. Marlee looked like she was short-circuiting.

Ada's face lit up. "You guys beat us here?"

"In a shocking turn of events, yes. Look, even Lazy Jerry beat you girls," Sanjay teased.

Marlee's amber eyes met Jericho's and he waited for the irritated blaze to ignite there, but instead, she looked almost impressed. Lena came over, giving Jericho a side hug. August and Ada talked loudly, but Jericho didn't pay attention to what they were saying. Until Marlee chimed in.

"Alright, you got me. But it ain't happening again."

Sanjay hung an arm over her shoulders.

"You know we love you right? Even though you're psychotic?"

The glare she shot at her friend as she crossed her arms reminded Jericho so much of his younger sister that it made him feel a little homesick.

Marlee reached up, patting the side of Sanjay's face roughly.

"Sure, and I love you guys even though he's a dumbass and you're a twerp."

August wrapped his big arms around both Marlee and Sanjay earning a high-pitched laugh from them both.

"Dude, can't breathe!" Sanjay tapped August's arm.

Lena sat at one of the tables and seemed to enjoy watching the interaction. She glanced at Jericho.

"Are you drinking?"

His eyebrow twitched up.

"I'm in a room full of extroverts, is that a question?"

Lena rolled her eyes.

"I'll go get our tickets for putt-putt," August announced.

Ada followed him.

"Do they have different colored balls here?"

"Oh my god Ada, you can't just ask people what color their balls are!" August replied in a valley girl's voice.

Ada laughed loudly, smacking him on the arm as they headed for the mini golf register.

Sanjay and Marlee moved to stand next to the table Jericho stood at and Lena sat.

Holding out a hand to Sanjay, Lena introduced herself, "Hey, I don't know if we've met or seen each other on campus but I'm Lena. Lazy Jerry over here is my brotha from anotha motha."

Sanjay shook her hand, grinning.

"Sanjay. We might have crossed paths. Nice to meet you."

He elbowed Jericho.

"Yeah, Lazy Jerry is starting to grow on all of us."

"What the hell is this 'Lazy Jerry' thing about?" Jericho laughed lightly, trying to play off his concern as a joke.

Sanjay's thick brows furrowed as if he just realized how the nickname might make Jericho feel. His thumb jutted in the general direction of August and Ada.

"Oh Ada, she comes up with a really bad nickname for all of her friends until she finds a good one. It's kind of a rite of passage."

"It was my fault. I was complaining about you being late and it stuck." Marlee admitted, looking apologetic.

Jericho rocked back on his heels. "Ah. I guess, in that case, I share some of the blame since I was late."

He ignored the way Lena glanced suggestively between him and Marlee.

"So, what was yours?" he asked Sanjay.

"Bean Boy," Sanjay replied flatly. "Which then turned into Beanie Baby."

"It was cute," Marlee giggled.

Sanjay gave her a half-lidded stare.

She turned to Jericho and Lena. "Anyways. . . I'm gonna go

order some drinks. What do you guys want?"

"August will want shots."

Marlee sighed loudly, "If he wants to order that stupid BJ shot thing, he can order it himself."

Sanjay made a face.

"I never want to watch that again. We will just tell him they don't make those here."

"I don't know, sounds entertaining," Lena laughed.

Sanjay just shook his head.

Marlee looked at Jericho. "You want anything?"

"I could just order for myself."

"It's not a problem," she insisted. "Unless it's some off-the-wall cocktail that I have to write down."

A smile tilted her full lips.

"No," he laughed. "No, I'll just have a Guinness."

"Sanjay?"

"Rum and coke."

She nodded and looked at Lena. "Lena?"

"Whiskey."

"Okie Dokie."

And with that, she headed to the bar. Sanjay looked over toward Ada and August.

"I'm gonna check on the putt-putt status."

He sent Jericho and Lena finger guns with a laugh and headed in the direction of his other friends.

Lena stood up.

"You know what, I forgot to tell Marlee to make that whiskey neat. Can you go tell her?"

"Is that necessary?" Jericho sighed.

"Yes. What if she brings it back on the rocks? Then my night would be ruined."

Jericho frowned, gesturing toward the bar.

"Why don't you go up there?"

"Because I gotta poop, Jerry."

"Okay, stop—"

"I don't got a lotta time, man, this turtle is coming out of its shell."

Jericho covered his ears.

"Fine! Fine! Just go do your business."

He started for the bar.

Nasty woman.

He shook his head with a shudder. He'd known Lena since high school, so it wasn't all that unexpected for her to be so vulgar. But it still caught him off guard.

Especially in social settings.

Coming up beside Marlee, he leaned on the bar top. She gave him a curious look. He pushed his hair away from his face.

"Lena wanted me to make sure her whiskey was neat."

"Oh, okay, sure," she smiled as she tucked her hair behind her ear.

Jericho watched the movement, seeing the flash of her wishing flower tattoo again. He wanted to ask her about it but he couldn't quite get himself to.

"Thanks," he said, tapping the counter.

She nodded, holding his gaze. He nodded back, finally breaking away from the warm amber.

"Cool cool cool." And with that, he headed back out to their table.

He forced himself not to glance back over his shoulder. When he returned, the group was gathered at the table, talking about the scorecards they had been given.

Lena raised a brow, saying quietly to Jericho when he was within earshot, "What no blindfold this time?"

His neck heated, sending his friend a very tired look.

"Shut up."

"Girls versus guys," Ada announced.

August nodded.

"Yeah, bring it."

At that moment Marlee came back with the drinks and handed them out.

"What did I miss?"

"You, Ada, and Lena against Me, Jericho, and August,"

Sanjay explained.

She sipped her own drink and smirked.

"Oh, you guys are going to have your asses handed to you."

"Pride cometh before the fall, ma'am," August quipped in a funny voice before throwing back a shot.

Everyone grabbed a ball and a putter, heading onto the course with their drinks in hand. Coming to the first hole, Sanjay gave a mock bow.

"Ladies first."

CHAPTER NINE

Marlee

Marlee fixed the thin straps of her draping top and adjusted the long-chained drop necklace.

"Ada I need the queen of fashion to tell me this is okay!"

She turned, checking out the half-open back as a swell of nerves made her second guess every piece of her outfit.

Ada yelled out a muffled," Coming!"

And Marlee heard her jump over the back of the couch. She peeked in the door, but upon seeing her friend she came in the door.

"Damn, mami! The Queen approves. All of this—" she waved a hand around Marlee. "Is a YAS."

Marlee blushed, laughing, "Are you sure? It's not too much?"

"It's a party, why would it be too much?"

Marlee shrugged. "I don't want to be a try-hard."

Ada rolled her eyes, coming up behind her friend to look at her in the mirror.

"Who even cares if you are? Do you want to wear this?"

"Yes. . ."

"Then wear it. You look beautiful."

"Thank you," Marlee smiled as Ada's words calmed some of her nerves.

"Of course. But can I make a suggestion?"

Marlee's brow lifted. Ada took out the clip in her hair so that her natural curls fell down her back.

"Rock the lion's mane."

Marlee ran a hand through her hair and sighed, "Alright."

She smoothed the stretchy fabric of her black skirt.

"I should get going. Thanks again."

Ada pulled her into a hug.

"My pleasure. Now go have a good time. You deserve it miss try-hard."

Marlee snorted and the girls made funny faces at each other as she headed out the door.

Walking across campus in heels was one of her more stupid ideas. Halfway to the auditorium, her arches ached, and she remembered that shoes like these were torture devices dressed in a pretty package. And yet she was still wearing them.

Pulling out her phone she turned on the flashlight to make sure she didn't break her ankle by not watching where she stepped.

Even from outside the auditorium doors she could hear the music and the laughter of her peers celebrating their progress. They had put in so much work and after a successful table read, Marlee felt pretty confident about how this show would go.

She was grateful to be surrounded by all these people who shared her dream. Glancing at the time, she almost laughed. Here she was almost fifteen minutes early, and some of them had beat her to the party.

Parties at seven o'clock at night are way more fun than a class at seven in the morning for everyone but you, Marlee.

Inside, the auditorium had been decorated with personalized banners and balloons were everywhere. The music blared and people were already dancing and drinking.

Marlee waved at some of the cast members as she stopped by the cooler of drinks. Picking up a strawberry margarita, she made her rounds saying hello to people until she circled back to the front. She looked around for Jericho.

Is he going to be here?

"Hey, Marlee."

She turned toward Bennet.

"Oh, hi Bennet."

She remembered to smile as she stole one last glance at the doors.

He gestured around the room with his drink in hand.

"This is great."

"Yeah, the set crew did a great job setting this up. I'm so excited to see the mock-ups they're unveiling tonight."

"Right! Sounds like Jericho and his team really put in a lot of work into them."

She nodded. "I think they did."

He smiled as his eyes swept over her quickly.

"You look great by the way."

"Oh, thank you, so do you," she half-laughed.

"Thanks. Hey, I'll see you around."

He gently bumped her arm and headed for a group of cast members.

Looking at the clock she shook her head, a smile pulling at the corners of her mouth.

Of course, he's late.

Finishing the can of strawberry margarita, she tossed the can and poured herself some of the mystery punch.

This might be a horrible idea.

She shrugged and braced herself as she took the first sip. Almost coughing, she gave her cup an approving look.

Nice.

Out of the corner of her eye, she caught sight of someone coming in the door and smiled as she took another sip of the spiked punch. For whatever reason, she knew it was him and willed herself not to look in his direction. Not until he stepped up beside her.

Warmth started to spread through her.

It's obviously the alcohol.

Without looking at him, a genuine smile lit up her face.

"Late again, Byers."

"It's cool to be late to parties."

She could hear his returning smile.

When she looked at him, she was a little stunned by his appearance for a moment. His slightly unbuttoned, dark shirt was half tucked into his casual slacks with the sleeves rolled just enough to show off a bit of his forearm.

No paint in sight.

"Hmm," she hummed, dragging her eyes up to his face where his dark hair fell back from his face. But he wasn't looking at her.

"You don't agree."

"No."

He looked at her now, his sea-green eyes hidden by his lashes as they took their time over her.

"Hmm."

Marlee suddenly felt her very bones buzzing, the heat of the alcohol amplifying her blushing cheeks.

I imagined that. It's the alcohol.

She took another sip.

And then Lena was hooking her arms with each of theirs, pulling them along.

"Come play a game with us, guys."

Jericho started to object but Lena cut him off, "Don't be a party pooper, Jerry."

Marlee tried not to spill her drink or trip in her heels— or both.

"What game?"

"Spin the bottle or something," Lena answered and Marlee almost did trip.

She hadn't played a game like that since high school.

"Why that game?"

"It's fun, now sit."

Lena helped Marlee sit and then pulled Jericho to the other end of the circle of partygoers. She looked around the circle.

"Spin the bottle or. . .?"

"Seven minutes in heaven?" One of the guys, whose name was Chad if she remembered correctly, suggested.

And to her horror, the rest of the group agreed.

This is so much worse than spin the bottle.

Someone asked what the game was and as they explained the rules, Marlee threw back the rest of her drink.

"Who are we voting into the closet first?" She didn't give anyone even a second to respond before suggesting, "I nominate the director and lead set designer. Jericho and Marlee. All in favor, take a shot."

Jericho looked like he wanted to kill Lena, and as he glanced at Marlee she thought there was an apology in his eyes.

Marlee felt like she was in a dream, watching almost the entire group take a shot. The majority was obvious.

Fuck.

Lena pointed to the small broom closet nearby with a wink.

"And if we refuse?"

"You take off a piece of clothing. Accessories don't count."

Marlee's eyes widened.

Considering that besides her underwear, she really only had her skirt and top, that was a hell no. Jericho's jaw tightened as he stood up and walked over to offer a hand up.

Taking it before she could talk herself out of it, she followed him to the closet as the group hooted and hollered behind them. Marlee was pretty sure her whole body was blushing.

As they entered the closet, which was similar in size to the last closet they had been stuck in together, her heart hammered against her ribcage. Jericho closed the door behind them, and at least the sounds of the group were fairly drowned out.

She looked up at him.

"I didn't think I would be stuck in a closet two times in my lifetime, let alone in one month."

"Yeah . . . I'm sorry about her," he sighed, shifting and his chest accidentally brushing up against hers.

She took a breath.

Why does he smell so good?!

"It's fine," she said quietly.

Her feet were killing her already. She moved, trying to

somehow kick them off but only succeeded in losing her balance. Her hands grabbed handfuls of his shirt.

"Ow— sorry," she giggled as the brooms she had knocked him back against rattled loudly.

"You, okay?" he laughed softly as his hands held above her hips to steady her.

"My feet are killing me. I don't know why I wore these stupid shoes," she mumbled. Glancing at him she couldn't help how red her cheeks were as she asked, "Can I hold onto you so I can take them off?"

"Sure."

She ignored how the roughness of his reply made her feel.

Moving her hands to his shoulders she made sure she didn't look him in the eyes, reaching back as she lifted her foot as much as she could and pulled the shoe off. Switching sides, she repeated the movements to remove the other. She flexed her painted toes against the cool floor and sighed.

Her eyes lifted to his, forgetting her plan entirely. Their eyes danced, gazes colliding and dropping and weaving for a moment.

Marlee cleared her throat. "So, what now?"

That tiny, confused wrinkle she had come to know so well formed between his brows.

"What do you mean?"

"I don't know, I just thought that we would have to present proof that something actually happened in here."

Feeling a little hazy and warm she rubbed her fingers against his tense shoulders, pinching the fabric of his shirt.

She watched his Adam's apple bob.

"You don't have to prove anything to them. Nothing *has* to happen, Marlee."

He dropped his hands away from her hips and she instantly missed the weight of them.

"You don't want anything to happen?"

She thought she had only been thinking that, not saying it out loud. But she was having a hard time separating her thoughts and her actual words now.

He didn't look like he knew what to say to that question. She didn't know why she asked.

"That was a stupid question, never mind. How many more minutes do we have?"

"Six."

This will be the longest seven minutes of my life.

CHAPTER TEN

Jericho

Jericho couldn't bring himself to answer her question aloud.

I don't want to have *to do anything. She has no idea what I want. I don't know that I even know. But if something is going to happen, I want the wanting to be mutual.*

He almost wished she would take her hands away because he could barely stand how the simple, comfortable touch was unraveling him.

When she looked up at him again, he studied the full pout of her lips, the dark frame of her eyelashes around the warm amber of her eyes, and the delicate dusting of freckles across her nose and up her cheekbones. The wispy curls that kissed her face made his fingers itch with the urge to wrap them around.

Her lips parted slightly as her eyes studied him back. Both looked almost afraid. And Jericho was, at this moment, afraid of what he wanted.

Marlee was clearly intoxicated after the mystery punch, so he decided that this was the only reason for her to be so comfortable in their current situation.

It's the alcohol. If she were sober, she would be complaining about the cramped quarters. Probably even scolding me about Lena's behavior.

He almost smiled.

"What are you thinking?" Her whisper made his heart race.

"Too much," he whispered back.

Her thumbs brushed lines along the collar of his shirt. His

eyes followed the full curls of her hair where they fell over her shoulder, glancing where, if she were to lean just a little, they would be chest to chest.

He had tried not to notice earlier how her draping top drew gentle attention to her soft curves. However, in their current state of proximity, it was impossible not to acknowledge.

She's so beautiful.

"Well . . . stop thinking," she demanded, carefully tugging on his collar.

His breathing hitched as her chest pressed against him.

Fuck.

"Marlee—" he warned in a rough voice.

But her hands were already past his shoulders as her arms loosely circled his neck, bringing their faces dangerously close. Heat rushed up his neck and the softness of her body alone made him hard.

"You don't want to kiss me," he breathed.

"I don't?"

She stared at his mouth as her fingers teased the ends of the hair at the back of his head. Her eyes lifted and she tilted her head— studying him with hazy eyes.

"I'm the bane of your existence, or did you forget? And you're tipsy."

"I never said you were the bane of my existence."

"You didn't have to."

He was desperately searching for something to make her irritated with him— anything to bring her back to earth to stop torturing him like this. She looked genuinely confused by his words, but not angry.

Shockingly, she didn't even take the bait to argue. She swayed a little and even though her hold on him kept her from toppling, Jericho's hands instinctively came to her waist again.

"You frustrate me," she said, almost like a caress as her fingers kept tugging at his hair.

He practically groaned at the prickling sensation it sent over his scalp. His hands squeezed her sides, fighting not to pull her entire body to his.

"Please, stop," he pleaded.

If we don't get out of this closet right now—

"You really don't want to kiss me."

She sounded disappointed and started to drop her arms as her cheeks turned an even darker shade of pink.

"Sorry—"

A knock sounded at the closet door, and someone called out that their seven minutes were up, making them both jump. Jericho felt the rush of mingling emotions fill his chest. But he couldn't sort through a single one— not here.

I need to get out of here.

Taking Marlee's arms away he moved past her, mumbling an incoherent apology as he breezed past the group of partygoers and made a beeline for the door. And he didn't slow down until he got back to his dorm. Clumsily unlocking the door he shut it behind himself, pressing his back to the cool surface and finally taking in a deep breath.

Did that just happen?

For a good fifteen minutes, Jericho paced, trying to sort out how he felt and trying to justify or debunk those feelings with what he thought to be logical explanations.

He had almost convinced himself that everything had happened because of the alcohol involved when an uneven knock sounded at his door. He froze, thinking he had imagined it.

But it came again, and he moved to the door to open it.

On the other side was Marlee, her heels in her hands as she swayed a bit on her feet.

Why did she follow me back?

"Marlee?"

She proceeded to chuck the heels into his apartment, narrowly missing Jericho as he flinched.

"What was that for?" he asked incredulously.

She pointed at the shoes, though it looked like she was pointing at Jericho.

"Those... devices of torture were designed by the devil."

She shoved Jericho back into the dorm room.

"Marlee—"

"I have blisters on my blisters, dude."

She tried to pull a foot up to show him, hopping around funnily before almost falling.

Jericho steadied her, grinding his teeth.

"You need to leave."

She clutched his arms and looked up at him with big eyes.

"You're strong."

"Ohhkaaay, I think you had too much mystery punch," he remarked.

She frowned. "No."

He rolled his eyes.

"Seriously, I didn't! I know my limits."

"Clearly." Jericho guided her to the couch and made her sit down. "Don't move."

She didn't object, watching him as he went into the kitchen, pulled out one of August's giant water bottles, and began filling it with water and ice. Then he put a piece of bread in the toaster. While that was toasting, he brought her the water bottle.

"Drink some water, Marlee."

She took the water bottle and eyed it.

"This is a big ass water bottle."

"August."

She studied the sticker on the side that read 'I don't sweat, I sparkle' and giggled, "Right."

She started taking sips, pulling one of the pillows on the couch to her middle. The toast popped so Jericho went back and put it on a plate, and grabbed an avocado from the basket of fruit they had on the counter to spread some of it on top.

"You're not allergic to avocado, right?"

She responded with a giggly, "Noooo."

"Cool."

He brought it over, placed it on the coffee table in front of the couch, and then sat down on the other end. She stared at him, taking another sip of water but frowned at the toast.

"It will make you feel better, trust me."

"What do your tattoos mean?"

She hugged the water bottle, leaning her head on the couch cushion. Jericho paused, unsure why she would ask, though, in general, it was pretty normal even for strangers to ask him about his tattoos. She pressed her fingers to her own neck.

"Like, what is the significance of the death moth?"

It was the easiest for Jericho to explain, so he relaxed a little. He ran a thumb over the ink at his throat.

"Might sound silly, but it was a really important lesson for me to learn that, even if it looked or felt scary, I needed to be myself no matter what."

She drank more water. "I like that."

They smiled at each other.

Jericho wasn't sure why he felt so comfortable sitting here and talking with her. She seemed to be just as relaxed, but he was still a little on guard— waiting for her to be bossy again or start getting frustrated with anything he did or said.

"And the others?"

"Which ones?" he asked slowly as he was unsure that he wanted to share all of those details.

She set the water aside and scooted next to him, reaching out a tentative hand to push the collar of his shirt over. His heart rate picked up as her fingers just barely brushed the tattoo on the front of his shoulder.

"What animal is that?" she asked.

He couldn't move or take his eyes from her as the moonlight from the window behind them cast a glow over the curves of her face.

Why didn't I turn on the lights when I came inside?

"I don't know." He cleared his throat of the husky tone and continued, "No one knows . . . the figure was found painted on the wall of a cave in Indonesia— some say it's 50,000 years old. One of the oldest known, figurative art pieces in the world."

"Wow."

She pulled her hand away and Jericho let out a slow breath.

Trying to steer the conversation away from himself, he brushed her hair away from the wishing flower tattoo behind her ear.

"What about yours? Why a wishing flower?"

"Wishing consumes just as much energy as planning," she recited with a funny smile.

"My mom always said I was a dreamer and that it was a good thing, but then she would scold me about how dreams are accomplished by actions and not wishes."

"So that's where you get it," he teased.

The water must be clearing her head. She sounds a little more like herself.

Marlee shrugged, flashing him a shy grin as she reached for the toast, turning it ninety degrees on the plate.

"I would argue with her that I could have my bundle of wishes and *make* them come true. And then she would ruffle my hair and say, 'that's my girl'."

Taking one bite of the toast, she put it back and snuggled deeper against the cushions and, to Jericho's surprise, him.

"That's cute," he commented.

"My head hurts."

"Drink more water."

"Look who's bossy now."

"It's just a suggestion," he smirked.

Her answering laugh was what made Jericho believe that they were no longer enemies.

CHAPTER ELEVEN

Marlee

After an oddly comfortable stretch of silence, Marlee turned her face up to look at Jericho. He tore his eyes from staring out the window to look at her, his brows twitching upward.

"You didn't finish telling me about your tattoos."

He looked hesitant.

"What does the one on your ribcage say?" She pushed herself up so that her head rested on the cushion by his shoulder.

She tried not to look as eager as she felt to know these little details. And as he shifted his body toward her, she almost lost the battle.

At least, that was what she thought, because it really did show on her face how interested she was.

"One word from you would silence me forever," he answered, almost looking embarrassed.

Something inside her heart almost burst.

"I don't believe you."

She loved Pride and Prejudice.

This must be a joke. Is he trying to make fun of me?

And suddenly she was back in high school where the boy she trusted used any means possible to gain her trust only to take from her.

"You're joking," she gave a nervous laugh, pulling back.

Jericho frowned.

"Why would I joke about that?"

He sounded so serious that it pulled her back to the present. *This isn't the same.*

"So, you actually like Pride and Prejudice?"

"Yes." He eyed her. "Do you?"

Suddenly, her mind flashed back to just a week ago when she had made herself a nest of blankets and eaten half a tub of cookie dough ice cream while watching the movie. She had gotten a 99% on one of her exams. It had been unacceptable. And Pride and Prejudice was her go-to comfort movie.

"Of course, I do. What kind of woman would I be if I didn't?"

She sounded so defensive that Jericho stared at her. She stared back. Then the tension broke, and they both laughed lightly.

Marlee tilted her head, tugging at the ends of her hair.

"Can I see your tattoos again?"

"Again? When did you—" he cut off, obviously remembering the mishap in the closet. "Oh, right. Um."

He ran a hand through his hair, his eyes dropping away.

"Oh c'mon, don't act like you're shy now."

He crossed his arms, and she realized how demanding she sounded.

Her cheeks heated.

"Please?"

Watching him contemplate her request made her curious about what went on in his head. And just when she was going to back down and tell him not to worry about it, he let out a breath.

"Okay." He stood, an amused smile tilting his lips. "Since you said please."

As he started unbuttoning his shirt Marlee suddenly felt like she was hot and cold at the same time. With his head slightly bent, the sections of his dark hair at his temple tumbled forward and the moonlight from the window shone on every inch of skin that he revealed with each button taken down.

She was pretty sure she had never been at a loss for words in her life, but right now she could only think about how beautiful he was.

He set the black button-up on the table and half turned so she could see the cursive quote that wrapped one side of his ribs. She sat up a little straighter, her eyes appraising the ink.

"Ok, I believe you," she teased.

He rolled his eyes but smiled.

"Why that quote?"

"Because . . ." he trailed off, looking shy as he sat back down. "Well, because it's iconic. But it also just resonated with me personally."

Marlee nodded, feeling that he was being vulnerable with her even if he didn't explain that statement. She gently rested her knee against his leg.

"I get that. It resonates with me too. Something about the way Darcy says it just— it's almost comforting. Because he is giving Elizabeth the power to say whatever answer she chooses and he would just accept it."

Not push and plead and guilt trip her into a yes.

She met his eyes which were full of so many unsaid things she was afraid to look away and miss a single one, even if she couldn't understand the words.

"Yes. Exactly," he agreed quietly.

Her gaze moved to his mouth and something inside her heart stirred and gravitated toward him. Somehow, they had ended up on the same side of the couch, so close their shoulders were brushing and her knee was comfortably touching his leg. And all Marlee knew was that somehow it wasn't enough.

"Why didn't you want to kiss me?"

It was a quiet, vulnerable question. One that she might regret later, but Marlee was much too curious. And she was too tired of pretending to ignore whatever this push and pull was between them.

"When did I say I didn't?" Jericho murmured.

"It didn't seem like you wanted to."

He let out a breath. "You were intoxicated."

"Well, I'm not now," she countered softly.

He didn't say anything to that, only studied her as if he could somehow tell if she was lying. And while she wasn't intoxicated— thanks to him taking care of her— she was still quite buzzed.

Her heart raced as she leaned closer, her gaze dancing between his eyes and mouth.

Maybe this is a bad idea...

but then he shifted so slowly and carefully that their lips hovered just agonizing centimeters apart.

"Are you sure?" he whispered.

She was surprised she even heard him over the pounding of her heart.

Her lashes almost fluttered closed.

"Yes," she breathed.

Her fingers hooked behind his neck, feeling his racing pulse beneath her thumb as she lifted her chin. When his lips met hers so gently, she knew that if she had been standing, her knees would have surely buckled underneath her.

Goosebumps prickled her skin.

At first, she had planned only to kiss him briefly and get it out of her system.

Just one kiss, Marlee, was what she had told herself.

But she tilted her head to deepen the kiss instead, and his hand came to the side of her neck as he tilted the opposite way. He pulled gently at her neck. She leaned, and their gentle kiss turned into a deep, searching dance that left Marlee short of breath.

Breaking away, her chest heaved, and the amber of her eyes smoldered from under her lowered lashes. Jericho's sea-green gaze was hazy as his fingers dug a little deeper into the back of her hair.

And it was the only invitation she needed as her other hand lifted to his shoulder to pull herself over to straddle his lap. Her skirt rolled up on her thighs, but she didn't care as her hands pushed into his hair and kissed him again.

His hand was aggravatingly polite as it stayed at her knee,

so Marlee took hold of it— guiding his touch along her thigh and then around to her back. And as she rocked her hips against his, he groaned against her mouth.

His fingers tangled in the crisscrossing straps of her top as he pressed his hand into her lower back, grinding her center against his hardening cock.

Marlee's breathing shuddered as a desperate whimper came from her throat.

Jericho's teeth caught her bottom lip, slowly tugging it as he pulled back and let it go. He didn't waste any time before leaning back in to trail slow kisses along her jaw.

Pausing when he reached the furthest point, he tugged at the back of her hair so that her head fell back. Marlee's hands gripped his shoulders, her hips still grinding as Jericho's tongue danced over her skin.

Her face warmed, aching heavily as each grinding stroke wound her tighter. "Fuck," she moaned breathlessly as Jericho's mouth moved down the curve where her shoulder met her neck.

And then he was shifting and leaning her back down on the couch.

Hooking his thumb under the strap of her top he slipped it off her shoulder and murmured against her skin, "Is this, okay?" She nodded, wrapping one leg around the back of his.

His lips painted slow strokes across her skin, pulling the strap further down as he went. Her nails scraped up his back and over the ridges of his shoulder blades— earning a deep hum of approval from Jericho.

"Won't August be home soon?" Marlee asked, even though she wanted to forget everything but how her body felt underneath Jericho.

The last thing she needed would be for her old high school buddy to walk in on her banging his roommate.

"No, I don't think so," Jericho answered distractedly before kissing her mouth again.

Marlee kissed him back, almost losing every thought in her head.

"Take me back to your room?"

He hesitated, his fingers brushing at her skin.

"I don't know… is that really what you want?"

"If it wasn't, I wouldn't ask," she whispered. "Is it . . . what *you* want?"

It felt like his eyes caressed every curve of her face. "You have no idea how much I want that right now."

The way he blushed as he said it had Marlee captivated.

With their hips pressed close, a soft, shy laugh danced on her words, "I think, *maybe*, I have an idea."

"You don't."

His voice was rough.

"Then show me, Jerry."

CHAPTER TWELVE

Jericho

Even as they left the couch, neither one of them stopped touching— their bodies moving toward Jericho's room in a dance of light touches and pulling and pushing set to the music of Marlee's sighs and Jericho's bated breath.

Clumsily pushing through the door, he felt Marlee's fingers grip the band of his pants. His fingers pulled at the tangle of straps at her back as his foot pushed the door closed.

As he backed her up to the edge of his bed, Jericho's hands carefully took down the straps of her shirt. With how loose the ties in the back had become it slipped down and over her hips to settle on the floor at her feet— leaving just the thin, lace bralette she wore.

Marlee unhooked the button on his pants, looking up at him as she slipped her palm down against his aching cock. He bit back a groan, lifting a hand to caress one of her breasts as he unzipped the front of her skirt with his other hand.

They tossed the clothing aside.

Her arms came up around his shoulders as she lifted her lips to his. His shoulder dipped and his arm circled her body— enjoying the warmth of her skin under his fingers and against his body as he leaned her backward onto the mattress. He felt her tongue slip against his as his fingers pushed under the thin fabric of her bralette to tease her peaked nipple.

When she arched into the touch and her hands dug into his hair, his hand at her back unhooked the bralette clasp. In a swift movement, he pulled the garment off.

Trailing his hand along her soft curves and down the line of her stomach he tugged at her underwear, but Marlee's hands pushed against his chest— breaking the kiss.

"Do you have a condom?"

He glanced at his bedside table.

"I should . . . somewhere."

"August probably has a shit ton. Just borrow one of his."

"*Borrow?*"

He started to laugh.

Marlee smacked his shoulder as her face reddened.

But she laughed, "You know what I meant smartass."

"Ow."

He grinned, going quickly to the bathroom where August usually kept an extra box or two under the sink. Grabbing one, he smirked.

I'll throw a few quarters at him later for it.

When he came back into the room, Marlee had removed her underwear already. He shifted the condom between his fingers as he took in the full sight of her.

She's so fucking sexy.

She walked over, holding out her hand. He tilted his head and placed the package in her palm. Her eyebrow rose just a little.

"Lose the boxers, Byers."

And still bossy as hell.

He was starting to realize that, maybe, he liked that about her a lot more than he realized.

Doing as she asked, he smirked when her eyes couldn't seem to decide where to look and took the package back from her. Grabbing a corner with his teeth he ripped it open. Marlee smiled, giving a half-roll of her eyes.

Admittedly, Jericho didn't have a lot of experience with sex, but he knew enough that he felt like he should have been able to put the condom on without a problem. But of course, he would have trouble in front of her.

"Do you want me to—" Marlee started to ask.

Feeling embarrassed he shook his head.

"No, it's okay."

She came closer and he was suddenly nervous, not willing to look at her.

What if she starts laughing at me?

But before his thoughts could spiral further her hand gently came to the side of his neck, pulling him down for a soft kiss.

"Let me help," she whispered close to his mouth, their eyes locked for a moment.

Her fingers gently took the condom from him and as she got down on her knees Jericho felt like his brain was short-circuiting.

The sight alone was enough to make him rock hard, but as her hands worked the condom over him, he resisted the urge to curse out loud.

She stood up, looking like she was about to say something but upon seeing the blush painting her cheeks Jericho's hands reached to cradle her face and brought her mouth back to his. Marlee made a soft sound of surprise as her hands came to his ribs.

Walking back a few steps, he helped her back into the position they had been in before, one hand moving behind her knee to pull her leg up against his hip. As his head teased against her arousal, Marlee's nails dug into his skin. He pressed closer, stroking her with his hard length as his hips arched forward and back.

Her breathing shuddered.

Dipping his chin to break their kiss, he rested his forehead against hers, reaching down to notch himself against her entrance.

He looked into the heated amber of her eyes, asking with a rough, almost shaky voice, "Are you ok?" She nodded; her mouth parted slightly.

"You can still tell me to stop—"

"Don't stop," she interrupted softly, lifting her leg just high enough on his hip so that his head sank into her velvet entrance.

Jericho's breath rattled in his chest, the heat of her slowly pulling him deeper until he was sheathed inside her.

Fuck, she feels so perfect.

The whining moan that came from Marlee's throat sent shivers through his entire body. Pushing his fingers under her head, he held the back of her neck, tucking his forearm under her shoulder. Her hands pushed up his sides, hooking her arms around his shoulder blades so that her fingers gripped the tops of his shoulders. Their eyes met as the ends of their noses brushed.

Gripping her leg, he started into a rhythm— going slow at first as if waiting for Marlee to come to her senses and tell him to stop. But she didn't. She held onto him, her chest rising and falling against his.

With each stroke and with every sound she made, he throbbed inside her.

Her nails bit into his skin.

Their breathing quickened.

He thrust deeper.

Marlee pleaded in hushed, dirty tones—

"Faster. . .Harder. *Yes*. . . Slower. *Fuck*. . . Right there."

And Jericho did all of that and more— every command she murmured, he obliged. Each one was tinder added to a bonfire waiting to be lit.

He bent his head next to hers, the softness of her breasts pressed against his chest as he started to chase his release. And so did she as her other leg lifted to hook around his hip, pulling him deeper.

"*Marlee*," he groaned, thrusting harder.

Her teeth found his ear, biting down gently as she moaned. He could barely focus on keeping rhythm as the pleasure began to overwhelm his senses.

And then Marlee was pushing his shoulder, guiding him onto his back. He started to ask if she was okay, but her mouth sealed over his in a breathless kiss as she seated herself fully on him.

Oh damn—

When she pulled away, he let her take his hands and pin them under her own. And the sight of her with wild curls and flushed cheeks, the bright amber of her eyes watching him as she rode his cock— he started seeing colors. He suddenly wanted to dedicate an entire canvas to her.

Her hips rolled against his, gaining momentum as she held his hands down. She started to shudder, her mouth falling open and her fingers starting to slip.

Sensing she was on the edge; Jericho freed his hands carefully and reached up. The pads of his fingers brushed along her jaw and back into her hair. His other hand curled around her neck.

Searching her eyes and being careful not to be rough, he waited for any sign that she didn't like what he was doing. But her hand came to his wrist, and her head started to fall back.

As she rocked her hips harder and faster, his breathing stuttered, and the heaviness of his release started to peak. Tugging at her hair and neck to bring her closer, he brushed a heated kiss over her chin.

One more roll of her hips and her nails dug into his wrist, a moaning cry coming from her throat. Her other hand gripped his bicep as she rode out her orgasm. And Jericho could not hold back any longer as he came with a force he hadn't known before —his rough groan mixing with her cries as they exhausted their pleasure.

CHAPTER THIRTEEN

Marlee

Waking up in Jericho's bed was not as strange as Marlee had expected. And that fact made it more terrifying than anything. Shifting under the blankets she breathed in and rolled to her back, rubbing her hands over her face.

She pushed her hair away from her forehead and stared at the ceiling, though she wasn't seeing anything but how Jericho looked underneath her when she was riding him.

She covered her blushing face, her quiet voice muffled by her palms, "Fuck."

She hadn't meant to sleep with him.

Shut up, yes you did. You've been thirsting for weeks but can't even admit it to yourself.

She sighed, rolling her eyes. Their passionate kisses and every touch kept replaying in her head— reminding her body of the chemistry between them.

And apparently, between my legs, she thought as the dull ache began to throb again.

Dammit, what was I thinking?

Sitting up, she threw aside the covers and glanced at the alarm clock on his bedside table.

8:07 AM.

Her eyes widened. She never slept past seven. She stood up, panic coursing through her as she thought she was late for class. But it was Saturday. Which meant she had no excuse to rush out of Jericho's dorm.

And most definitely no excuse to get on his ass for making her late or something of the like to hide behind.

Some clanging sounds coming from the kitchen made her peek through the crack in the door. She froze, her heart fluttering.

He's already awake. Cooking...

She tried to ignore the fact that he was shirtless and obviously just out of the shower. She chewed on her thumbnail as a thought occurred to her.

He's probably making us breakfast.

And that sent Marlee into a full panic. It was too much all at once on top of the fact that she was a little shocked by how things had escalated between them.

Steeling herself, she stepped out into the living room, crossing her arms over her chest. Her eyes darted toward the door. She thought to make a mad dash immediately but talked herself down.

Stay calm. Just say you have to get back and study or something.

As she got closer, he flipped whatever was in the pan. She cleared her throat.

Jericho looked over his shoulder, a tentative smile tilting his lips.

"Hey."

"Hi."

She tucked her hair behind her ears as she leaned on the countertop.

He pointed to the sizzling pan.

"I'm making some breakfast. You okay with grilled cheese? It's kind of my specialty," he laughed lightly.

She couldn't help but smile.

"Grilled cheese for breakfast?"

"Why not?"

He smiled fully, turning back to move the grilled cheese onto a plate.

"Uhm. You know, it sounds great, but I should really get going."

She started to move toward the door. She had to leave now, or she was afraid she would jump his bones again. Everything that he did or said made her feel things that she wasn't willing to face yet.

He paused with the plate in hand, that stupidly adorable wrinkle forming between his brows. But before he could say a word she was already at the door.

"See you at the next theater class," she quickly added and opened the door, ready to bolt.

But there stood August.

Key in hand.

Blinking at her.

"Mar?"

"Hey buddy!"

She started to push past him. He held up his hands as she moved into the hall and one of his eyebrows quirked up.

"Hi, bye!"

Marlee didn't stick around to hear what he said in return as she broke into a full-on power walk through the halls and down the stairs of the frat house. She passed a few of the guys, but they didn't pay her much mind.

Probably used to girls coming and going like this.

She hoped. She didn't need gossip to start up— especially with the scout coming.

She forgot to avoid the corner of campus where Sanjay set up his coffee cart. Seeing him she took a hard left straight into the bushes to try and avoid him. The branches and leaves scraped at her skin.

"Ow— *shit,*" she growled, trying to shove them away as she tried to navigate the foliage.

"Marlee, what the hell are you doing?" She heard Sanjay call out.

She froze, her brain racing for an explanation.

"Uh— I . . . I dropped something over here last night."

"You need help?"

"No!"

Hastily picking up a small rock she held up her fist.

"I got it!"

And then she took off again. She was jogging across campus. Which, most days, was a very Marlee thing to do if she were late. But she didn't think that even then she had busted ass like this.

The elevator ride up to her room could have been compared to torture. Even though there were no other students inside with her, she was just waiting for a bunch of girls from her dorm house to show up and judge her. Or worse, try to trade war stories with her because they would know exactly what she had been up to.

Miraculously, she only passed one or two girls, but they were too busy to notice her.

Getting up to the door she looked at the rock in her hand, realizing that she had left her purse and her keys at Jericho's.

"No. No. No. No!"

I'm such an idiot.

She held the rock's cool, smooth surface to her forehead. She hoped Ada was awake because there was no way in hell, she would run all the way back across campus. Gritting her teeth, she bumped her fist against the door continually.

She closed her eyes, whispering, "C'mon, Ada, answer the door."

She lost count of how many knocks she was on by the time she heard her friend yell, "Okay, okay! I'm coming."

Marlee tugged nervously at the ends of her hair as the lock clicked and Ada opened the door.

"Dude it's eight in the morning what—" Her grey eyes widened, glancing over Marlee. "Marlee, where the heck have you been?"

"I slept over at a friend's place. Drank too much."

Desperate to be somewhere safe, she pushed past Ada and headed for the bathroom.

"Who?"

"You don't know them."

She cringed inwardly. She hated lying to Ada, but she was too embarrassed to check herself.

Ada scoffed as they entered the bathroom, "I know all your friends, Mar."

"Not this one," she replied hastily, turning the shower on.

"Is that Jericho's shirt?"

"What?" her voice was way too high-pitched.

She looked down.

She was, in fact, wearing his shirt.

And his boxers.

I ran across campus in his boxers. August and Sanjay saw me wearing Jericho's clothes.

Her face flamed as she looked at Ada.

"*Marlee.*"

"Uhm."

One corner of Ada's mouth lifted, opening as her eyebrows rose.

"Did you guys. . ." She made some crude gestures as she started to giggle excitedly, "Wham bam thank you, ma'am!" If it were possible, Marlee's face reddened further. And it was all the evidence her best friend needed.

"Oh my— you *did*!"

She couldn't move or get herself to deny it. And her lack of enthusiasm made Ada's smile falter.

What's wrong, Mar?"

"I left all my stuff there."

"Everything?" She blinked. Marlee nodded. "So, you just left wearing his clothes?"

"Yup."

"Was he still asleep?"

"No."

There was a pause.

Ada seated herself on the counter.

"Was it really bad?"

Marlee fought with herself. She tried to convince herself that she didn't remember all that much. She had to have drunk a lot for this to happen.

Right?

Liar.

She tried to shove the intoxicating memories into the recesses of her mind.

"I don't remember much. We were both pretty drunk."

Obviously. It had to have been the alcohol.

She turned around, taking off the borrowed clothes. She subconsciously brought the shirt to her nose— breathing in the faint scent of acrylic paint and the same laundry detergent he had used on her other shirt.

Realizing what she was doing, she tossed the shirt into the garbage can as if the action could rid her of all the feelings she suddenly had.

"Oh." Ada sounded concerned. "Are you okay?"

Marlee stepped into the shower, letting the water run over her face for a moment. She didn't even know the answer to that question.

"I'm fine."

It was a robotic answer, even to Marlee's ears.

"Are you sure? You're acting weird."

Marlee heard her jump down from the counter. "Wait, it was consensual right? He didn't—"

"I remember him asking," she interrupted. "And I remember saying yes."

"Okay, good. But are you *sure* you are good?"

"Uhm— ask me after my shower."

"Mar. . ."

Sitting down on the floor of the tub, she pulled her knees to her chest and closed her eyes.

"I appreciate you checking on me, but right now I think I just need to be alone. I need to work through it in my own head."

And convince myself that I didn't just make a huge mistake.

"If that's what you want. I'll be here if you need me."

Ada left, shutting the bathroom door.

Marlee's eyes stung.

"Fuck..."

CHAPTER FOURTEEN

Jericho

It had taken Jericho a moment to recover from Marlee bolting out the front door so abruptly. But eventually, he took a breath and threw a half smile at his friend.

He set the plate on the counter and ran a hand through his hair as his eyes dropped away from August's questioning gaze.

"Hungry?"

August shut the door, dropping his bag in the entryway.

"Uh, sure."

He looked back at the door, frowning. "Wait, why was Marlee here?"

Jericho rubbed his jaw, hesitating to answer. If Marlee had been so quick to leave, he wasn't sure that she wanted her friends to know about what happened. Or anyone else, for that matter.

He didn't know how he felt about that. But the way his gut was twisting, well, it wasn't good.

August picked up the grilled cheese, holding it up and raising a brow.

"This wasn't for me, was it."

Jericho bit his lips together and shook his head. His friend looked slightly shocked as he gave a slow nod. Sitting down on one of the bar stools he took a bite of the sandwich.

"So, do you wanna talk about it?" he asked around his food.

"I don't know," he answered with a frustrated laugh.

He felt like, maybe, he needed to talk about it because he

was confused. He had no clue about how to read Marlee Firth-Diaz. She was the one who followed him home. She had made the first move.

And then she ran like she couldn't get away fast enough.

He let out a frustrated sigh.

"It's . . . complicated." Jericho felt his neck heating.

August nodded.

"Yeah, she is." He took another bite.

"Yeah." August was staring at him as if patiently waiting for him to spill his guts.

"I don't know if I should talk about this with you," Jericho finally admitted after a prolonged silence.

"Did something—" he cut off, his eyes studying Jericho and then the counter as if he was putting all the pieces together.

He looked back at Jericho.

"She was wearing your clothes."

Jericho averted his eyes to the counter, tapping the spatula against it as a shy smile tugged at the corners of his mouth.

"Dude."

"Dude," he echoed in a heavy voice, still feeling like he couldn't just come out and tell August what had happened between him and Marlee.

"Hey, if you don't wanna talk about what happened, that's cool. Just want you to know I'm here for you bro."

August held up his hands.

"Thanks, man." Jericho smiled, setting the spatula in the sink.

Bumping his fist against the counter he couldn't get himself to leave the kitchen.

Or to leave this alone.

"Should I go after her?"

August tilted his head, slowly starting to shake it.

Jericho ran a hand through his hair.

"I mean she just left, and we didn't really talk after— after everything." He cleared his throat, deciding to stop talking. He was pretty sure he was turning red in the face.

August shifted, looking slightly uncomfortable.

"No, I think it's best to leave her be. At least for the rest of today." He rubbed the back of his neck. "I don't know what happened—" he held up a finger— "And I'm not asking! But Marlee needs time."

"How much time?"

"I don't know, just don't push her. She has a habit of running away when she feels pressured," he answered, giving Jericho a serious look.

"Alright," Jericho sighed, grabbing the hand towel from the counter, and balling it in his hands.

August stood and patted him on the shoulder before picking up his bag. When he headed for the bathroom, he turned and pointed over his shoulder with his thumb.

"Please tell me you didn't defile the shower, Jerry."

Jericho rolled his eyes, starting to blush again.

"Oh my god, don't tell me it was the countertops too!"

Jericho chucked the towel at August's head with an embarrassed laugh. August ducked, a broad grin lighting up his face.

"Dude, if you guys break the couch, it's a dealbreaker for me."

"Fuck off, Gus!" Jericho laughed.

August was laughing too, waving a hand at his friend before closing the door to the bathroom behind him. Jericho shook his head and walked back to his room.

After shutting the door, he glanced around, his eyes getting caught on his mussed sheets. He had honestly thought she would be up at the crack of dawn, ready to go get coffee or something. But he had gotten up before her.

She must have slept well then.

He glanced at the floor, his eyes slowly following the trail of clothing tossed here and there. And it finally registered in Jericho's brain that she had run out of there in his clothes.

He picked up her clothes, pressing the fabric under his nose as he closed his eyes.

She likes to be prepared for things, she probably really needed to study or something. I shouldn't worry about it.

He put the clothes on his bed, planning to wash them for her later. Moving to his dresser he grabbed a navy shirt and pulled it over his head. He had his internship with the tattoo artist, Keiran, who was mentoring him today.

They had an arrangement so that Jericho could come into the shop at any time as long as it was a Saturday and stay as long as he wanted. Usually, he would go in the evening, but he didn't think he could climb back in bed after last night and go back to sleep.

Grabbing a sweatshirt and hooking a hair tie around his wrist, he shut his door and went to grab his keys. By the door were Marlee's purse and heels.

She probably needs her purse sooner than tomorrow.

He threw his keys and caught them. So much for giving her space. Picking up the purse and heels, he locked the door behind himself and started the walk toward Marlee's dorm.

"Hey, Lazy Jerry!" Sanjay greeted as Jericho passed.

He smiled, lifting the hand that held his keys.

"What's up, Sanjay?"

But the guys didn't continue the conversation as Sanjay was currently busy with a very long line of students, and Jericho was on a mission.

He was surprised at how short the walk seemed, but he knew it was quite a way from the main buildings compared to his own dorm. He was about to open the doors when a group of girls almost ran into him.

"Sorry—" he apologized as they giggled and shrugged it off, sticking close together and talking quietly and loudly simultaneously.

He shook his head and entered the building, pausing at the elevator as he realized he had no idea what floor she was on.

Dammit.

Stuck awkwardly waiting for another girl to come by whom he could ask, Jericho rocked on his feet.

Finally, two girls came out of the elevator. And though talking to strangers generally made him want to throw up he made himself ask, "Uh, hey, can I ask you guys something?"

They paused, turning toward him with confused frowns.

"Sure?" one of the girls said slowly.

"Do either of you know which floor Marlee Firth-Diaz is on?"

They exchanged looks he couldn't read.

"I just want to give her these." He held up the heels and purse as he continued quickly, "She left them at a party last night."

They looked at Marlee's belongings and one of the girls nodded at the other who held up three fingers.

"She's on floor three, room 4C."

"Thanks."

He pressed the elevator button for floor three as the girls walked away.

Just drop them outside the door and text her they are outside. You don't have to knock on the door.

The elevator doors opened, and he stepped inside, tapping his foot as it took him up to the correct floor. He couldn't stop thinking about the conversation they had about their tattoos. Or any of their conversations for that matter. The way she tucked her hair behind her ears or when she actually smiled at him.

Fuck, I just want to keep talking to her.

But August had advised him to give her space, and he knew Marlee longer than anyone else, so Jericho was going to trust what he said.

When the doors opened, he walked down the hall and set the purse and heels at the door. He pulled out his phone and sent Marlee a text. It was kind of odd, considering how they only had each other's numbers because of the play.

There were a few random texts from her requesting things for the set. And Jericho's responses were primarily questions or one-word affirmations of the things she asked. So, sending this message to tell her he had left her personal belongings outside her door struck him as funny. Because it really looked odd next to their other messages.

He sent the text and then knocked three times before walking back down the hall. And as he stood in the elevator, waiting for the damned doors to shut, her door opened. It felt like his heart both stopped beating and went into overtime as she picked up the purse and heels and then looked down the hall.

Their gazes collided just as the doors started to shut.

Jericho gripped the bar along the wall of the elevator to keep himself from jumping to stop them.

And he didn't let go until the elevator had stopped on the bottom floor.

CHAPTER FIFTEEN

Marlee

It wasn't that she had been dreading the next theater class, but in a way, she had been. Her stomach was in knots. And she hadn't even been able to stomach her coffee that morning.

Marlee had thrown herself into the work that needed to get done as her team helped to set up to rehearse their songs. But for all her avoiding and nerves, she had wound herself up for no reason because Jericho was cool as a freaking cucumber.

They even argued a little about how to position one of the backdrops. And she had caught him smirking when he had walked away. Marlee had struggled to keep herself from smiling. But no matter the chemistry between them, she had already tried to convince her brain that their relationship could not continue.

Not with the scout coming.

She was the director.

He was the set designer.

End of story.

Colleges...

Who slept together.

She shook her head, scribbling aggressively in her notes.

"Marlee?"

"What?" she snapped before looking up.

Then she realized who had spoken and Marlee immediately closed her binder to send Lena an apologetic look.

Taking a breath, she pushed her hair behind her ears.

“Sorry, how can I help you, Lena?”

"We need you to approve some things over in set design."

She looked more amused than put off by the director's mood.

Marlee glanced over, seeing Jericho talking and gesturing with his hands.

"I can look it over after class."

Lena raised a brow

"If we don't get approvals for these, we can't move forward."

"Okay,” she relented. “I'll be right over."

You talked to him earlier. You can do it again. You're a professional.

She almost snorted.

Lena gave Marlee a thumbs up. "Cool, thanks!"

Did she just wink at me?

Marlee sighed with a shake of her head and gathered her binder. Bracing herself, she headed over to set design. She tried to act nonchalantly even though her heart was racing as she stepped up to stand beside Jericho.

“Hey, Jerry,” she greeted.

When he looked over at her with a lopsided smile, butterflies zinged through her body.

Stop blushing, Marlee. Stop.

“Hey, Marlee.” More butterflies.

She gripped her binder a little tighter, turning her attention to the projects.

"What did you need approvals for?"

“The backdrops for the last act. We have mock-ups ready—I just want to make sure you like them.”

She blinked her gaze back to him.

They're already wrapping up the projects for the last act.

Maybe she shouldn't have been surprised. Because even though he had been late those few times, it hadn't affected his work. Or the quality of it for that matter. Those butterflies were starting again, and Marlee tried not to be distracted by them.

"You guys are doing great keeping up with the schedule."

"Trying our best." He inclined his head. "Do you wanna see the mock-ups?"

"Yeah, sure."

He started for the backstage door and Marlee followed. As he opened the door for her, she almost hesitated.

Truth be told, she was afraid that once she was alone with him her resolve would crumble. But she needed to make some things clear, and it was probably best done in private anyways.

"I can't believe we almost have the entire set ready," Marlee commented as she moved through the door.

Jericho nodded, walking her back to the mock-ups.

"Yeah. Turned out to be more fun than I thought it would be," he laughed lightly.

Waving a hand toward the project in front of them, Jericho looked at her.

"Here they are, boss."

Studying the mock-ups, she almost wanted to fall back into nitpicking every detail of his work, but he had really outdone himself with this set.

So, all she said was, "Approved."

"Just like that?"

She looked at him, crossing her arms.

"Yes. Is there a problem with that?"

"No. I just expected more pushback," he admitted.

Marlee shifted her weight from one foot to the other. She didn't think she was that hard to work with. Then again, even she cringed to remember some of their interactions.

"It looks great. I'm excited to see the finished product."

He smiled.

"Thanks."

She nodded, hugging her binder.

"Oh, hey, I meant to give this to you earlier, but it just wasn't the right moment." He rubbed the back of his neck and held up a finger. "Wait here."

"Okay," Marlee laughed nervously, watching him as he went behind the set.

When he came back with a bag in hand, her brain raced through the possibilities of what it could be.

He held out the bag.

He's blushing.

Her heart picked up speed as she took it and peeked inside.

Oh.

Now Marlee was blushing. He had brought her clothes back, and they were definitely laundered.

And folded nicely.

"I figured you would want those back," he joked, meeting her eyes.

She broke away from his gaze, looking at the clothes instead.

Her face flamed.

"Thanks. Uh I— I didn't bring yours."

Why is he so nice? Fuck.

He crossed his arms. "That was my favorite shirt, Marlee."

"It was covered in paint stains."

"Memories. Not stains."

Jericho stepped closer, tilting his head.

"I painted a masterpiece in that shirt," he told her in a serious tone, so close that she could smell his cologne. She opened her mouth and then shut it at the way his eyes were lit up.

Marlee lifted her chin.

"Could it really be a masterpiece if there was more paint on you than on the canvas, Byers?"

One corner of his mouth lifted as he brought his hand up. She froze as his thumb brushed gently over her bottom lip.

"In the hands of a good artist, a single stroke can be a masterpiece."

"I guess, you would know," she replied quietly.

He studied her, his thumb tracing a line along her jaw.

"I had a really good time with you, after the party."

Marlee shivered.

Jericho's eyes dropped and as he started to lean in, she began to panic. And even though she couldn't deny the chemistry between them, she told herself that it just wasn't a good idea. So just when his lips were about to meet hers, Marlee dipped her chin away.

"You know, there was a lot of alcohol, and we were all hyped up on how much progress we had made for this production," she said, unable to look him in the eyes.

But she felt that old tension start to build up between them again as he took a step back, dropping his hand away.

"And it's probably not a good idea for the director and the set designer to be mixing business and— and pleasure," Marlee continued, her knuckles turning white where she gripped her binder.

"I mean, I don't really remember a lot." And even though she knew the words were harmful, and not the truth, she couldn't stop herself from self-sabotaging.

She had never let herself let go like she had that night. She had goals and milestones she worked toward, but Marlee never allowed herself to take a breather and just live. And for whatever reason, Jericho made it easy to set down her lists, and relax.

If she were honest with herself, she would realize that she was terrified of that.

When she finally looked up, his face was wholly unreadable but with the way that his jaw ticked she knew he was probably angry.

He ran a hand through his hair.

"Sure, yeah, you're right."

He started to back up, and it took all her strength not to take back everything she had said as a pit started to bottom out in her stomach.

But she watched him go without another word. And when he turned his back and walked out the door, Marlee pretended that she didn't feel his absence like a musical without the ballad.

Gathering the shreds of her self-respect she headed back

into the auditorium, taking the door on stage left instead of the right where Jericho had exited.

CHAPTER SIXTEEN

Jericho

"This is getting ridiculous, Jer," Lena sighed as he handed her a list of things for Marlee to read over.

It had only been two days since their backstage chat, and Jericho was still avoiding any interaction with her. Poor Lena had been the middle man, or rather woman, since. She whacked him with the paper.

"You should talk to her again."

He shook his head and lowered his voice, "I think she's made it clear that this is strictly a working relationship."

"You know business relationships also require communication, right?"

He sent her a tired stare and Lena shoved the paper into his hands again.

"No, dude, I'm not your secretary."

She waved a hand. "Act like an adult and handle the consequences of your actions."

"Lena—"

"Boy, bye," she laughed, walking away, and leaving Jericho with the list.

He groaned, half crumpling the paper in his fist. He was still reeling from the shock of Marlee's words the other day.

She didn't remember much.

In truth, he was confused and hurt, but mostly he was beating himself up about the whole thing. Even though he had asked— making sure she gave consent for everything that happened— if she had been too drunk to remember, it didn't matter.

And he felt like shit about it.

I thought we both had a great time. I mean, she gave no indication otherwise . . . until she ran out the morning after.

This was why he didn't interact with girls much. Things always got complicated.

Taking a breath, he looked at the paper, contemplating if he should just hand her the list. He wouldn't have to talk at least. He tried to smooth it out but ended up just balling it up and stuffing it in his pocket.

There was a lot of commotion going on around him, speakers were being tested as well as lights. The crew was putting the finishing touches on the props and backdrop. And Marlee was at the helm of it all, calling out instructions with a hand on her hip.

Truly, it didn't help his situation that she looked so good in her glasses and little blazer. As if sensing his staring, she glanced over and caught him with the blazing amber of her eyes. She tugged at the bottom of her curls and Jericho tore his eyes from hers.

Clenching his fist and then flexing his fingers, he walked away to stage right, hoping that his crew would need help with something.

"Bennet don't worry so much about your footwork— you're just chasing each other around the garden. Talia, just a little more projecting of that killer vibrato on the end of your notes," Marlee instructed.

Jericho leaned against the edge of the backdrop, crossing his arms. There wasn't much to do but watch the actors perform, so a few of the art students on the design crew sat in a huddle close by, whispering and doing the same as he was. And he was impressed so far with the talent of their leads.

Marlee came up on the stage, showing Talia and Bennet some of the steps again, and then handed them each a water bottle.

"Hydration is important, guys," she told them with a semi-stern look, but as they took a drink and conversed, she smiled again.

When the music started, she waved at the guy who oversaw the sound booth.

"Woah, wait, wait!"

He immediately shut it down and she headed for stage left.

"Are we good?" Bennet laughed.

"Yes! I'll be back here."

She gave him and Talia a thumbs up.

"Okay, one more time, from the top!" Marlee called out, clapping her hands. Jericho tried to keep his eyes on those performing and not her as the music started, but he couldn't stop stealing glances.

"There's something sweet, and almost kind. But he was mean, and he was coarse and unrefined," Talia's rich voice trilled. *"And now he's dear and so unsure. . . I wonder why I didn't see it there before."*

Keeping his eyes forward didn't last long, as he suddenly felt the heat of her gaze on him. But when he glanced, she averted her eyes back to Talia and Bennet.

Bennet's baritone filled the auditorium, *"She glanced this way, I thought I saw. And when we touched, she didn't shudder at my paw . . . no, it can't be. I'll just ignore. But then, she's never looked at me that way before."*

Their eyes seemed to be dancing just as much as Talia and Bennet were across the stage. But as Talia sang again, neither one of them seemed to be able to look away.

"New and a bit . . . alarming. Who'd have ever thought that this could be? True that he's no prince charming . . . but there's something in him that I simply didn't see."

Jericho was the one to tear his gaze from hers, and as the people playing Mrs. Potts, Cogsworth and Lumiere began their part of the song, he turned and started for the exit. He couldn't handle all of the tension let alone all the feelings that he was having to face.

Lena asked him where he was going, but he just waved a hand and kept walking toward the doors.

But before he made it out of the last exit, Marlee pushed through the doors he had just gone through.

"Jericho, wait!"

He paused, debating whether to turn around or keep walking. Their last conversation kept playing in his head for the past two days, trying to figure out what had gone wrong.

He had thought, maybe, they were just wrong together but Jericho didn't think they had even had much of a chance to figure that out. And he had tried to work out why he felt that his feelings had been reciprocated before she had said those things.

He was still confused why she acted like sleeping together had been a mistake when she had been making the moves.

And here she was again, chasing *him.*

He half turned to look at her, deciding to give her a chance to tell him the truth. Because he was convinced that she was not just lying to him, but to herself.

But until she told him as much, he wouldn't make any moves.

She came closer, her cheeks flushed as she tucked her hair behind her ears.

"Leaving so soon?"

Is she really about to scold me?

He sighed, "There's only like twenty minutes left of class, Marlee—"

"No, I'm sorry, I'm not— that's not why I asked you to wait."

Her blush deepened.

He frowned, watching as she tugged at the ends of her curls.

She's nervous.

"Do you have a minute?"

He looked around, hooking his fingers over the back of his

neck.

"Sure, but if this is about what happened, we don't have to —"

"Will you go on a date with me?" she blurted.

He blinked once.

Twice.

Did she just—?

There was a rise and fall of excitement in Jericho's chest, but it was quickly washed away by doubt.

"Why?"

"Well, you know, to see if that night was really just the alcohol," she explained.

He stared at her.

"Call it a fake date, if you want! I just— I need to know."

"I don't know, Marlee."

He didn't like the idea of going on a *fake* date. Things already felt so complicated.

I'd rather it be real even if it didn't work out.

"We can do whatever you want. But if you don't want to try a date, that's fine," she started to backtrack, and Jericho could see that she was losing her nerve.

"I don't want to go on a fake date."

Marlee twisted her hair around her finger.

"Okay, then just a date?"

He crossed his arms, trying to lighten the mood by teasing her, "What's in it for me?"

"Food? Hopefully good conversation," she laughed, blushing again.

He was starting to think she actually wanted to go on a date with him.

"Okay, I can get with that. But what about you?"

She blinked.

"What about me?"

"What's in it for you?"

"A second chance," she offered quietly. "If you can give me one?"

He thought about that for a moment, but he had already made his decision. Giving her a lopsided smile, he nodded.

"I think I can do that."

CHAPTER SEVENTEEN

Marlee

"So, you guys are going on a date?"

Marlee pulled her hair into a ponytail, looking at Ada. "Yes. We already went over this."

"Yeah, I know. But honestly, I'm confused Mar. You guys, like, hated each other. And then you had hate sex and now you *like* him?"

Her face flamed as she tied off the ponytail.

"Oh my god, it wasn't hate sex."

Ada pursed her lips and then started to smirk.

"Mhm."

"What?"

"You like him." She didn't answer right away, making Ada squeal, "You do!"

"He's a nice guy, okay! And he's kinda hot, so."

She put some finishing touches on her makeup.

Ada snorted.

"*Kinda.* The dude's a smoke show."

Marlee sent her friend a surprised look.

"What? I got eyes, just because I see a nice ball doesn't mean I wanna smash it."

"What?!" Marlee laughed.

Ada was always making up funny volleyball euphemisms.

"I'm just saying— don't go out with him just because he's good-looking."

Marlee sobered a little.

"It's not just that, I promise."

Ada held up her hands, relenting just as there was a knock on the door.

She frowned at Marlee.

"You told Sanny we are postponing our movie marathon, right?"

"I texted him, yeah."

She headed for the door with Ada at her heels. But when she opened it there wasn't anyone there.

"Okay . . ."

Her friend peeked around her.

"There's a box."

Looking down where Ada was pointing, Marlee bent and picked it up. Turning it over in her hands, she found her name in one corner. Not written but painted in clean, even lettering.

Jericho?

"Oh! Is that from him?"

Marlee didn't answer, bringing the box back into her room to set it on the bed. She hesitated.

Ada was shaking her shoulders. "Open it!"

"Okay, okay!"

She playfully shoved her friend away and opened the box. Inside a soft yellow fabric peeked out around a notecard set in the middle. Picking up the card she read what it said out loud to Ada, "Be my guest. See you in an hour. Jericho."

Well, that's cute as hell.

"Ooohh!"

Setting it aside, she pulled the fabric up and unfolded it. She held up the yellow sundress and shared an impressed look with Ada. Marlee pressed the dress to her body, swaying a little.

"There's something else in here, Mar," Ada pointed out.

Marlee reached in and pulled out a simple chain necklace. The girls inspected it and Ada sat on the bed.

"Damn, the dude has game *and* style."

Marlee nodded emphatically.

Maybe this date was a bad idea. What if I like him too much?

She half rolled her eyes.

That's stupid. Isn't that what you want?

She really didn't know.

When she exited the elevator, she had not expected to find him waiting in the lobby already. Jericho stood up from where he had been seated.

He was sitting and waiting for me. He was definitely early.

She would be lying if that didn't make her feel something. Walking over she gave a gentle spin to show off the dress he had picked out for her.

He smiled.

"Hey, it looks good on you."

"I didn't peg you as a fashionista, Jerry, but you have good taste. I'll give you that," she replied, unable to stop her smile.

"I have some hidden talents."

"Hmm," she hummed, studying him.

She took note of the clean white T-shirt and navy-blue button-up he wore over it.

No paint in sight.

"So where are you taking me?"

"A few places."

She eyed him but he only smiled— giving up nothing.

Jericho held out his hand.

Marlee tried not to blush as she slipped her fingers into his. And she really tried not to think about the fact that she had already held his hand before this.

In a completely different context.

Sans clothing—

Marlee's cheekbones turned pink, and she had failed.

As he walked them out to the parking lot, she was a little unnerved by how comfortable she felt simply walking beside him. And when he stopped in front of a Ford pick-up truck, Marlee was sure he was joking.

"You good?"

"Yeah, I just didn't imagine you driving a truck."

He cocked his head, looking amused.

"What did you expect?" Jericho asked as he unlocked the passenger door and opened it for her.

"A motorcycle or something, I don't know. Just not a truck."

He leaned his head against the door frame, his eyebrows quirking up as he watched her studying the vehicle. She stepped up beside him to get into the truck but paused.

On the seat was a single rose and in the cup holder was a coffee, with familiar markings on the cup. She looked at him, fighting the urge to kiss him for being so thoughtful.

"Are you trying to kiss my ass, Byers?" she teased softly.

His eyes lit up.

"Of course not."

Butterflies.

When she was safely seated in the truck, he closed the door and walked around to his side. Her fingers brushed the soft petals of the rose as he hopped in. Marlee watched him start the engine and keep his hand on the gear shift as he backed out of the parking spot.

She brought the rose to her lips.

"You really won't tell me where we are going?"

"No."

The corner of his mouth twitched— keeping his eyes on the road.

She shook her head, acting disappointed, but surprisingly she didn't mind the mystery. The morning sun flashed through the passing palm trees as they drove down the busy streets.

Marlee set the rose safely on her lap and took up her coffee. Taking a cautious sip, she was impressed he had gotten her order right.

Sanny probably told him.

It still made her smile.

As they pulled onto a road marked with a sign reading, 'Point Sal State Beach', Marlee looked at Jericho curiously, but her eyes were drawn out the window again when the ocean came into view.

She hadn't been to the beach in a while. Since the term started. But over the summer she usually came down with August and Sanjay and they would surf while she read a book in the sun. A few times, Ada tagged along, and the girls would try to catch a few waves with them. Marlee hadn't ever gotten the hang of it, but Ada was a natural.

Jericho parked the truck and glanced at her.

"Feel like a walk on the beach?"

"Sure." She nodded, going to put her coffee in the cup holder.

"You can bring the coffee if you want."

"I might get tired of carrying it."

"Well, just let me know when and I'll carry it for you."

Marlee raised an eyebrow, smiling.

He mimicked her expression.

Dammit, he's adorable.

"Ok, Jerry, let's take a walk then," she laughed.

Down on the beach, the sand was already warm under the soles of Marlee's feet. She swung her sandals gently in one hand and sipped her coffee.

The waves bubbled up the wet sand, not quite reaching where Jericho walked beside her.

"Why did you think I drove a motorcycle?" Jericho asked, squinting against the bright, early afternoon sun.

"You look like you drive one."

She shrugged.

He dropped his hands in his pockets.

"Not everyone who has tattoos rides a bike, Marlee," he half laughed.

She pursed her lips.

"It wasn't the tattoos."

He looked at her funny, their arms bumping into each other.

Something in his expression changed.

"Oh, let me guess, it's because you think I'm irresponsible, right?"

Marlee cringed and looked at her feet. She had thought that. Before she had gotten to know him.

"I don't think that anymore," she clarified.

She braved a glance over at him. His face was still hard to read.

With an embarrassed laugh, she apologized, "Sorry I was such a bitch. I've been so stressed about this production, I let it get to me. But I shouldn't have lashed out at you."

"It's okay— I mean it isn't *okay*, but thank you," he replied.

The next wave that rushed up the shore rolled over Jericho's feet. But the icy water had barely kissed Marlee's toes when she shrieked, jumping away.

Jericho laughed, "You good?"

"The water is freezing!"

He tilted his head, his eyes lighting up. And then he kicked some water at her— the frosty droplets biting into the backs of her legs.

She screeched, running further away before he could send another volley.

He was grinning and Marlee couldn't help but smile back.

"What's wrong?"

"Jerk," she laughed.

"Come back." He placed a hand behind his back. "I promise I won't do it again."

"Liar."

"That's not nice," he teased.

Marlee took a few cautious steps back the way she came, her eyes narrowed on Jericho.

"You better not do that again, Jerry or I swear I will dunk your ass."

His dark brows rose, disappearing into the tousled hair on his forehead. Little did he know she had every intention of getting him back whether he tried to splash her again or not.

And when she was close enough she did just that— kicking her foot into the next wave to send an icy spray across his torso.

She didn't wait to see his reaction but she heard the laugh and knew he was coming after her as she ran. It didn't take him long to catch up.

Marlee laughed loudly as his arms came around her from behind, pulling her kicking feet off the ground as he started to carry her toward the waves.

"Wait— no! Jericho put me down!" She screamed.

Her hands clawed at his arms, trying to get a good grip in case he decided to drop her. And she kicked her heel into his shin.

"Ow!"

He laughed, and just when she thought he would drop her, he turned and walked her back to a safe spot. And as soon as he set her down, she spun and shoved her hands into his gut— sending him backward until he fell on his butt in the wet sand.

Her hands covered her mouth, trying to stifle her laughter as he stood up and looked back at the sandy, wet seat of his pants.

For a moment she was afraid she had gone too far as he stared at it, but then they both burst into laughter.

CHAPTER EIGHTEEN

Jericho

"It's not that bad," Marlee giggled.

"It's bad."

Jericho started to shrug out of the button-up he had on as an overshirt. She was still laughing out apologies as she reached out, trying to brush the sand away— patting at his ass. A laugh jumped out of him as he swatted her hand away.

It actually wasn't that bad, and he was willing to bet it would be dry before their next big stop. Or at least, be unnoticeable. He tied his extra shirt around his waist, not caring if it looked funny.

As they headed back up the beach, he was surprised when she slipped her hand back into his. Jericho glanced at how her fingers fit between his and tried not to smile.

A part of him had expected her to end the day early and declare that their relationship is only business. But she looked like she was having fun.

Marlee handed him her coffee cup. It felt empty. He held it up.

"Want me to toss this?"

"If you don't mind," she replied sheepishly.

He smiled and veered off toward the trash can that sat next to the bathrooms. Throwing it away, he jogged back over to where Marlee was waiting on the trail leading up to the parking area.

He paused, glancing back at the beach.

"You ready for phase two?"

She tucked her flyaway curls back behind her ears, her eyebrows lifting slightly.

"Oh, there are phases to this date?"

Jericho nodded, deciding he would play the mysterious card again.

"I'm not going to get any information out of you, am I."

"No."

"Alright," she gave a deep, dramatic sigh.

He glanced at his watch.

It was just after lunch which meant they still had some time to kill. But he had a plan for that. He looked at Marlee.

"You hungry?"

Jericho peered up at the simple menu of the street taco truck. There were only three options, but he was having trouble deciding between the carne asada and pork belly. Marlee had already ordered her chicken tacos and fixed him with an expectant stare.

It might have been one of the reasons he was taking his sweet time.

"Just get them both."

"I don't know."

He smirked.

She shoved at his arm and he sent her an amused grin.

"Order the damn tacos, Byers," she snorted, shaking her head. But he didn't miss the smile that lifted the corners of her lips.

He clicked his tongue.

"So bossy."

She shoved him harder, and he laughed, "Alright! Alright."

Turning to the person taking their order Jericho stepped up and ordered the carne asada and some churros. Taking their food to a picnic bench he sat across from Marlee.

She dug in immediately and groaned around her food, "I fucking love tacos."

Jericho smiled and followed suit, making a mental note—*Learn to make tacos.*

She held a hand in front of her mouth as she asked, "What's your favorite food?"

"Food," he deadpanned.

She rolled her eyes.

"No, c'mon, humor me. What is the one food you would gladly survive on until you die?"

He thought for a moment, chewing a bite of his taco. "Probably grilled cheese."

"Good choice. Comfort food."

"What about you? Coffee?" he teased, taking another bite.

She huffed a laugh, "You think you have me pegged, huh?"

"Just a guess. Also, I think a world where you don't have your coffee sounds terrifying."

"Okay, fair, but also— shut up," she laughed, chucking a piece of chicken at him.

He held up a hand to defend himself, but the food bounced off his chest and he laughed from behind closed lips.

"My mom makes the best mac and cheese on the planet, and I would be so happy to eat that for the rest of my life," she told him, looking like she was remembering life at home.

Jericho loved his family, so seeing Marlee's soft spot for her own made him feel even better about this date.

"That sounds perfect."

"I should ask her to make it when I come home for the holidays," she commented, stacking her plastic fork on top of her plate.

"My mom would always make fried chicken on Sunday, and I would beg her to make extra so I could take it in my lunch on Monday. I'm definitely requesting it on Thanksgiving, forget the turkey," Jericho laughed.

She smiled, her amber eyes lighting up as she rested her chin on her palm.

"And where is home for you?"

Jericho finished off his taco, copying how she had stacked her utensils.

"San Antonio, Texas."

Marlee blinked, her eyes looking over him.

"Seriously?"

"Yup."

"You don't have an accent."

"My mom grew up in Louisiana and is the only one in my family who has a real southern accent. Not everyone sounds like that down there in San Antonio anyways. If you go east you'll find more of that twang," he explained, amused by her fascination as she listened intently.

"Did you grow up on a farm? Can you ride a horse?"

He laughed, "A ranch, and yes."

"So, you're a cowboy."

She eyed him, smiling funnily.

"It's not that weird."

She waved a hand.

"No, it's just surprising!"

"Okay, well, where are you from?"

"Northern Cali. Just a six-hour drive away from here to home. Super boring."

He shook his head.

"That's not boring. At least you are kind of close so you can visit home easily, right?"

She stacked their plates, looking down at her hands.

"Yeah, that is nice, though, my little sister wishes I were farther away, I'm sure."

"Little siblings always pretend not to like their older ones, but I bet she misses you."

She looked up at him, pulling her ponytail over her shoulder.

"You have siblings?"

"Two sisters and a brother, yeah."

Her eyebrows lifted.

"You're the oldest?"

He shook his head, smiling just to talk about them.

"My sister, Juniper, is the oldest. I'm after her. My brother, Josef is next, and then Jessa."

"Lotta 'J' names," she mused.

He laughed, "Yeah. What's your sister's name?"

"Gianna. But I call her G-money. She hates it," Marlee snickered.

"That's cute."

She shrugged, her cheeks starting to turn pink. Reaching over, he took the plates from her and got up to throw them away. Marlee picked up their drinks and followed.

"So, what's next?"

He crossed his arms, deciding to tease her again because he liked how pretty she looked when she was blushing.

"What do you mean? What if that was it? Not up to your standards, professor?"

Her cheeks reddened further, but she mimicked his pose instead of getting defensive and teased him back, "Not quite an A yet, Byers."

"I guess we will have to fix that." He winked, reaching to tug on one of her loose curls.

His knuckles just barely brushed her jaw as he pulled his hand away and Marlee's eyelashes lowered for a moment. Jericho's eyes dipped to her lips.

Damn, I wanna kiss her.

When she looked up at him again, their eyes did that fluttery dance and he wondered if she wanted to kiss him just as badly. Instead of waiting to find out or even making a move, he inclined his head toward the truck.

"C'mon the day isn't over yet."

CHAPTER NINETEEN

Marlee

Marlee had no idea where Jericho was taking her next, but she wasn't worried about it. She looked over at him, unable to stop smiling. The date so far had been really nice. She kept waiting for things to blow up, or for herself to start sabotaging everything, but she felt relaxed around him.

She remembered thinking that he didn't care about a lot of things when they had first met but hearing him talk about his family or the way his eyes lit up when he was sharing music with her on the drive, she was starting to see that he did care.

And deeply. He was just quieter about it.

She looked out the window when he pulled into a parking lot, catching sight of the sign that read, 'Moonshine Flats'.

She'd never been, but it was a pretty popular bar.

What the...?

Turning back to him as he parked the truck, she tilted her head. She had said she wanted to find out what was between them without alcohol, so she felt a little nervous about this.

"What are we doing?"

Jericho reached behind her seat and pulled out two hats.

Cowboy hats.

He took the white one and placed it on her head. He grinned.

"Yee-haw or whatever."

A nervous laugh bubbled out of Marlee, "Jerry . . .?"

"We're going line-dancing."

He put the black one on and pointed at the bar. He must have caught her wary look because he assured her, "No drinking, just dancing."

She looked back at the bar.

When she was in high school, she had taken dance. But she hadn't done line dance before.

It will be fun. And we don't have to drink.

The thought of Jericho dancing was also kind of funny to her, and she was interested to see if he had yet another hidden talent.

When she met his questioning stare, her lips tilted in a soft smile.

"Well, cowboy, what are we waiting for?"

Inside, the music was already echoing around the bar and people were dancing. Marlee watched them move in unison, twisting and turning and laughing. She started to smile. Jericho walked forward, holding up a hand behind his back and glancing over his shoulder at her with an excited grin.

She reached forward, taking his fingers as a blush chased its way over her cheekbones.

He led her through the crowds to an empty table at the edge of the dance floor. She scooted closer, pulling his arm over her shoulder and they watched the dancing together. Marlee tracked the footwork, trying to get to know some of the moves.

Looking up at Jericho, she spoke loudly so he could hear her over the music.

"How will we know the steps?"

He leaned his ear closer and looked at her from under his eyelashes.

"Just follow my lead. You'll be fine."

Her eyes widened, glancing back at the dancing and then at Jericho. She wasn't sure about that. But she didn't have a chance to argue with him as the music fell away and then built into the next song.

And then Jericho was pulling her with him onto the floor.

Oh no—

He positioned her next to him and her heart started to beat faster.

As the beat started people began to move, it took Marlee a moment to gain confidence. But thanks to Jericho sending her encouraging grins and taking it slow next to her, soon she had her rhythm.

She followed his steps, getting a little distracted by how he looked in his white t-shirt and cowboy hat while moving like that.

Damn.

They were laughing and spinning now, almost touching as they moved. And then somehow, he ended up so close, Marlee hooked an arm around his neck. They swayed and stepped to the music, her head falling back as she laughed. She gripped the top of her hat with her other hand.

Jericho dipped her backward in a smooth move that made some of the onlookers cheer. Butterflies zinged through her body as his hand brushed along her lifted calf and gently held her knee to keep her from toppling.

She held onto the back of his neck as he brought her back up, getting caught in the sea green of his eyes for a little too long.

Kiss me, dammit.

Her eyes dipped but he didn't lean in and instead spun them into another dance. Marlee's skin felt a little like it was on fire. She wanted more of his touch.

And there was no alcohol in her bloodstream.

Marlee brushed the curls that had come loose at her temples behind her ears as they walked into Pizzarini. She probably looked like a mess from all the dancing. And she definitely had hat hair, but she didn't care. They had been laughing on the dance floor. It had continued during their drive as well— recounting some of the moments that weren't so perfect on the dance floor.

She had been a little surprised when they pulled into Pizzarini. But they had bomb pizza, and Marlee wasn't complaining. They slid into a booth after ordering a small pizza to share— half with the works and the other half with garlic chicken. Marlee unwrapped her straw and punched it through the ice in her soda.

"I did not know you could dance like that," she laughed before taking a sip of Pepsi.

He opened his own straw and threw the wrapper at her.

"Touché."

She grinned, batting the wrapper back his way. "Dude, that was so much fun. Do you go a lot?"

"August has gone with me a few times, but honestly it isn't as fun when you don't have a partner and your friend is stealing all the female attention," he laughed.

Marlee's smile softened, tilting her head.

She wasn't sure how Jericho could be overlooked, but then again, she had written him off at first too. She drew little designs in the condensation forming on her cup.

He watched her fingers.

"You think you'd go again?"

Marlee studied the way his eyelashes cast shadows against his cheeks. When he looked up at her she nodded.

"Yeah, I think I would."

"Cool."

"Cool cool cool," she giggled, watching him blush.

The waiter dropped off their pizza and it struck her funny that the last time they were at Pizzarini was right after their rude first meeting. And now they were here. Flirting. In the spirit of teasing, she didn't reach for a slice and looked at him expectantly.

Jericho paused, giving her a funny look.

"You good?"

She blinked innocently.

"Yeah, I just don't wanna make a hot mess."

Seeing the dots connect in his eyes as he started to shake his head and laugh made her smile.

"What, I need help, Jerry!"

He leaned on the table, looking thoughtfully over the pizza and then back at her.

"What kind would you like, professor?"

"One of each."

He raised his eyebrows. She rested her chin on her hands, fixing him with her best puppy-eyed look.

"*Please.*"

"Okay, since you said please," he relented and placed the pizza on her plate.

Her smile turned genuine then.

"Thank you."

When he reached for his own she swatted his hands away and served him two of the garlic chicken because that was the only kind of pizza he had touched that time all those weeks ago.

He laughed under his breath, "Do you want any of the other half?"

He shook his head.

"No, this is good, thank you."

They talked about the production, sharing ideas about the last details of the set. She found herself invested in every idea he had, and he listened to hers. Taking the rest of their pizza away in a box, they hopped back into Jericho's truck and Marlee sighed.

"So, is there a phase three, or were you just winging it today?" she asked as he started the engine.

With a confident little smile, he reached back behind the seat again. When he pulled out a binder, she frowned a little.

He handed it to her.

"Of course, there is phase three, I take this date business seriously," he responded.

Marlee opened the binder to a clean list of bullet points and outlines for where they were going or what they were doing. There were even neatly written notes about her coffee order and other details.

It rendered her speechless.

And if she had wanted to kiss him earlier, she definitely wanted to jump his bones now.

Heat rushed up her neck.

Reaching for the glovebox, she opened it and dug around until she found a pen. Jericho might have said her name or asked if she was okay, but she was on a mission. Going to the bottom of the list she made another bubble for the last bullet point and wrote, 'Kiss Marlee' there.

Then she closed it without even looking at what they were going to be doing next.

Jericho raised an eyebrow.

"What was that—?"

"You can't look yet," she interrupted, trying to bite back a blushing smile.

When he held up his hands, smiling to himself, she hugged the binder to her chest.

"I'm ready for phase three."

CHAPTER TWENTY

Jericho

When they had gotten to his dorm, Jericho, as he had planned, put Pride and Prejudice on. He could tell Marlee was excited and had even grabbed a blanket, half leaning against him throughout the movie.

In the end, they both teared up and Marlee smiled sweetly at him as her thumb brushed under his eye.

She half-sniffed, half-laughed, "The ending always gets me too."

She was so close that he, honestly, got a little distracted from talk of the movie. His fingers tugged at the ends of her curls, trying to focus on her eyes and not her lips.

"What did you write in the binder?" he asked.

Her eyes shifted away as she bit her lip.

"Just read it later."

When she looked back at him, he thought for sure she was waiting for him to lean in. But he was playing it safe and waiting for her to make any moves.

He didn't know how fast or slow she wanted to take the physical aspect, considering how they had started with that before ever going on a date.

When she got up, he did too, stretching his arms over his head.

"I always forget how long that movie is," he commented.

"Me too," she said, throwing the blanket over one of the couches.

She moved into the kitchen, seeming to be avoiding his eyes. He tried not to think much of it but when he moved around the counter, she crossed her arms and looked at her feet.

And he started to get nervous seeing the obvious shift in her mood. Jericho could feel her trying to put up that wall again.

In an effort to bring her out of her head, he leaned against the counter and tilted his head.

"Did you have fun?"

"I did," she told him, finally meeting his eyes. Clearing her throat, her hands rubbed at her arms. "Did you?"

"Yeah, I did." Jericho moved a bit closer.

At least she didn't back up.

Sensing that there was still something she was thinking too much about he asked, "Are you okay?"

She waved a hand, glancing at the fridge.

"Yeah, I'm good, um, does August have any beers here by chance?"

He felt his stomach drop.

After everything today...

He ground his teeth, running a hand through his hair.

"Maybe he does but— Marlee, I thought no alcohol was the whole point of this date."

"Yeah, but I—"

"You what? Can only stand being alone with me if you're intoxicated?"

He didn't care that he was interrupting her.

He was tired of trying to understand what she really wanted. And honestly, it hurt to feel like he was only tolerable when she was drinking.

"No."

"Then what?"

"I don't know," she started tugging at the ends of her hair.

"For weeks you have had more than enough ideas and things to say to me, but suddenly you don't?"

She looked at him, some kind of conflict in her eyes. She let out a breath, "I still don't know if this—" she gestured between them. "If it's a good idea."

He studied her, hoping that he would somehow be able to understand what was holding her back.

"You don't know if our relationship is a good idea?"

She nodded.

He stared at her.

"But getting drunk and sleeping with me is okay."

Her face reddened.

"No, Jerry—"

"I'm not interested in being your drunk booty call, Marlee."

She looked frustrated now.

Good, that makes two of us.

"That's not what that was. We were both drunk and things just escalated."

"I didn't even have one drink that night. And things didn't *just* escalate." Jericho took a shaky breath, "Dammit, I was so careful to make sure it was really what you wanted. . ."

He didn't want her to think he had taken advantage of that situation, but he really thought she had sobered up. She had answered all his questions coherently, and he had let her make a lot of the moves.

He met her eyes again, but she didn't respond— looking scared of whatever she was thinking.

"What do you want, Marlee?"

"I— I don't know," she stammered.

"I don't believe you." He stepped closer. "Do you like me, or was today just an act?"

She still didn't answer, and Jericho pushed on.

"Why aren't we a good idea?"

She pressed her back into the fridge as he came closer. "The production. We're basically working together."

His jaw ticked.

"It's a school production, Marlee. It's not that serious."

"It is to me," she snapped.

"Okay, but the talent scout isn't going to even see us together. All they will care about is the production."

She blinked away from his gaze.

"Getting buzzed and losing yourself in whatever this is between us for a few hours isn't going to change anything. It won't just go away."

Marlee looked back at him again, the heated amber of her eyes pinned to his mouth.

"Do you like me? Yes or no, just one word," he asked quietly.

Because if she said no, he would walk away. She wouldn't have to worry about him again, he would make sure of it.

He wouldn't even ask her why.

Jericho didn't know what he was expecting her to say, but he was not ready for how her hands grabbed hold of the collar of his shirt. She yanked his mouth to hers in a deep kiss and his hands pressed against the fridge door, caging her body.

She broke away, but her hands still held him close.

"Is that a, yes?" he asked breathlessly.

Their eyes danced and their noses bumped.

"Shut up—" she said as she pulled him back in for another kiss.

His hand came up to hold the side of her neck firmly, dipping his chin to break the kiss. Jericho pressed his forehead to hers, holding himself back just barely to make sure he heard her say it.

"Just one word, Marlee," he breathed.

She pulled at his shirt, her lips hovering near his like she couldn't keep away.

"Yes. I like you. *A lot.* Is that what you wanted?"

A smile flickered over his lips.

"Yes."

She lifted her chin to kiss him again, her arms pinned between their chests as he pressed his body close to hers. His thumb brushed over her ear as his fingers pushed behind her neck.

Her hands let go of his shirt, one pushing under the neckline and over his shoulder as the other dug into the back of his hair. Kissing away from her mouth, his hands tilted her head as he pressed his lips against the wishing flower behind her ear.

"Jerry?"

"Hmm," he hummed distractedly as he kissed her soft skin.

Her shoulder lifted and her hand fisted his hair.

"Do you like me?"

"You drive me crazy."

She let out a breathless laugh, "Is that a yes?"

"That's a hell yes," he said roughly, taking up her ear with his teeth and pulling.

"Even when I'm bossy?"

"Sometimes," he teased, smiling.

She gave his hair a playful yank and Jericho laughed, "See? That was kinda fun."

Seeing her blush, he leaned back in to kiss her. She started pushing him backward— her hands came down, tracing along his torso until she reached the hem of his shirt.

As his backside bumped into the counter, her fingers stole underneath, exploring every hard line and muscle from his chest back down to his v-line. Her fingers hooked around his belt, making him throb in anticipation.

And then she pulled away from the kiss, hesitating as her thumb tapped the buckle.

Gently pinching her chin, he lifted her face so he could see her eyes.

"What are you thinking?" he asked, heart racing.

Is she having second thoughts?

He didn't think he could take that.

But she started to smile a little shyly with hazy eyes, one hand brushing along his hip.

"That I wanna ride you until you can't remember your own name."

His balls tightened.

Oh, fuck yes.

"Good thing you brought your hat then, cowgirl."

CHAPTER TWENTY-ONE

Marlee

Pulling the hem of his shirt up, Marlee helped Jericho out of his white tee. She hugged her arms around his neck, one hand at the back of his head as she lifted on her toes to kiss him.

Unlike last time, Jericho didn't waste time being polite as his hands slipped down her back. Tilting her head to deepen the kiss she pulled closer as his hands gripped her ass. And then he was pulling her up and she was hooking her legs around his hips.

He walked them to the couch— carefully and slowly lowering them to the cushions. She shifted in his lap as he sat back. And then she started unbuckling his belt. Pulling it out of the loops she set it aside and looked back at Jericho.

Marlee studied the sharp lines of his face, the arch in his nose, and his deep-set eyes. His fingers made soft lines down her thighs as he tilted his head with a curious tilt to his lips.

He's aggravatingly beautiful, she thought as she smiled back.

Marlee traced her fingers gently over his features, leaving soft kisses in their wake. When he closed his eyes, she brushed over them with her thumbs and kissed his mouth once.

Then his jaw.

Her hands brushed against his temples as her fingers moved back into his hair. Tugging his head back to expose his neck, she moved her mouth over his throat, sucking and swirling her tongue over his tattoo.

And the way his breathing rattled spurred her on.

His hands moved up her thighs, under her dress until his fingers hooked in the waistband of her underwear. She rocked her hips against his erection, kissing the base of his throat.

The quiet, husky sounds he made vibrated against her lips. Her fingers loosened their hold on his hair— dragging her hands down his neck and shoulders and over his torso to the buttons of his pants.

His hands came back up to her neck, following the line of her collarbone and pushed the straps of her sundress off her shoulders as her fingers undid the button.

She helped him shift the jeans lower on his hips. Seeing the tattoo that had been half hidden there, she traced her fingers over the winged man that looked like he was falling from a bright sun.

"You never told me about this one."

She liked how rough his voice sounded as he answered, "It really didn't have much meaning. It's one of my original pieces. Inspired by the story of Icarus."

"Sounds meaningful to me."

Brushing her thumb over the ink and up his hip bone she met his eyes, saying softly, "You're so talented."

He visibly blushed.

"Thank you."

Her hands started to take down his zipper.

Marlee tilted her head, asking quietly, "Is this, okay?"

"Yes," he said, watching her fingers.

Lowering her eyes, she pushed the band of his jeans further down with his help. Lifting on her knees a bit she took his hard length in her hands.

Jericho groaned.

One of his hands hooked behind her thigh. His other fingers moved under her dress, slipping under the fabric of her underwear.

Marlee couldn't help but moan as he made slow strokes against her aching, wet heat.

She arched her hips against his fingers— stroking him in return with her firm grip. Feeling his eyes on her, watching how she reacted to each run of his fingers, Marlee's cheeks flushed. It was hard to focus when he was so good at that.

Jericho pulled her hips closer, taking his fingers away just enough so that he could hold her underwear out of the way. Her heart started to beat faster as he helped her lower onto him.

She let out a shaky breath when she had taken every last inch of him. His breathing sounded much the same, his lashes lowered and lips slightly parted.

Remembering something, she glanced back at the coffee table.

She didn't have to reach far to grab his cowboy hat and placed it on her head.

She smirked at him.

One corner of his mouth lifted.

And then his hands gripped her hips as he rolled his into hers. Butterflies rushed up from her core.

She matched his rhythm, holding onto his bicep.

"You're beautiful," Jericho murmured, bringing his lips to the exposed swell of her chest.

His words made her pick up momentum. Grinding harder. Her breath was coming faster.

His hands moved under her dress to take hold of her ass again. When he pushed and pulled with her, arching his hips as she rode his cock, Marlee's release started to build. Afraid she would come too fast; she reached for his hands and pulled them away— pinning them behind his head.

"Slow down, cowboy, I'm not done with you yet," she drawled in a breathless, sensual tone.

And then she kissed him, slowing her rhythm. Jericho's fingers curled around hers, kissing her back with fervor.

But as they broke the kiss and her forehead pressed against

his— her hands caging his wrists— Marlee rode him like she was chasing her next breath.

His whispered growls of encouragement made her ache around him—

"*Fuck.* Yes. *Marlee*, just like that."

The angle of her hips had him stroking her in all the right places and she knew she wasn't going to last much longer.

Her lips parted, trying her best to hold off. But even as she tried to draw out each roll of her hips, she was only wound tighter.

"Jericho—" she moaned, tumbling over the edge into pleasure.

She rode out the waves of her orgasm, panting as her fingers loosened their hold on his.

Now that his hands were free, Jericho slipped them out from under hers. Marlee flattened her own on his chest, locking eyes with him as he reached for her.

Her breathing hitched as he held her like the last time, she had ridden him— one hand fisting her hair and the other curling around her neck with just the right amount of pressure.

Her eyes almost rolled back.

Oh, hell yes.

He pulled her closer, his lips hovering close to hers as he rasped, "You make me so fucking hard."

And then he brushed a heated kiss to her mouth. Marlee whimpered against his lips.

She was caught up in the sea-green of his eyes as he thrusted his hips up against hers. Still so sensitive from her release, the friction worked a soft cry from her.

Jericho repeated the motion. Unable to think straight, she followed his lead— arching into him.

"That's it. Don't stop," he demanded.

She was a little surprised by how assertive he was starting to be. It was unexpected and so was the fact that she wanted more of that from him.

Rising to the challenge, her hand held his forearm as she

gained her momentum back.

"You gonna boss me around, Byers?" she asked, sounding out of breath.

His lips parted, eyes locked on her hips as she moved against him.

"Afraid I'll give you a run for your money?"

And then his eyes lifted to hers, the corner of his mouth twitching. "Somebody's gotta put you in your place."

Jericho's thumb pressed against her pulse, his voice lowering, "And I'm gonna enjoy the fuck out of it."

Marlee felt like her brain was short-circuiting. Between his words and his firm grip on her neck she was aching again.

Damn.

"Maybe I would like that," she countered, but her voice was thin, sounding more like she was pleading.

Jericho didn't miss a beat as his fingers caressed her wishing flower tattoo beneath her hair.

"Before we're done, you're gonna beg for it."

CHAPTER TWENTY-TWO

Jericho

The water from the shower cascaded over Jericho's shoulders as he pushed Marlee up against the wall. It pooled between her breasts where they were pressed against his chest, caressing her curves in rivulets much like his hands.

He could barely catch his breath between their kisses.

When Marlee's hands tried to shove between their hips, searching for him, Jericho pressed his body closer so she couldn't reach.

The frustrated, growling noise she made had him smirking against her lips. She pulled away, breathing hard.

"I wanna touch you," she pleaded.

He shook his head, gently bumping her nose with his.

"How bad?"

"What?"

As his hands smoothed up her sides, his erection throbbed against her thigh.

"Tell me how bad you wanna touch me."

"More than I want my coffee," she teased, the heated amber of her eyes warming him more than the shower could have.

That made him laugh, "That's saying something, I guess."

She nodded as her hands hooked over his shoulders.

But Jericho didn't plan to give in— not until she was

begging. His hands roamed down over her curves, flattening his palm over her stomach as he wedged his hand between them.

"I wanna touch you first," he told her as his fingers slipped between her legs.

Her nails bit into his shoulders as her breathing hitched. He almost groaned at how wet she still was and stroked slowly down her center— dragging his middle finger back and forth.

Marlee leaned her head back against the shower wall, moaning a muffled curse.

He watched her reaction to his touch as his fingers circled and stroked, falling away, and teasing her over and over. Jericho didn't stop until her breathing was rough and her legs were shaking.

She hung onto his shoulders, her wet curls clinging to her flushed cheeks as she pleaded softly, "Please— Jerry I'm so close —"

But as she arched her hips in search of another stroke of his fingers, he pulled away— bringing them instead to his mouth.

He didn't know what she was thinking, but he liked the way she blushed as he sucked her arousal from his fingers.

Seeming to gain a bit of clarity, she opened her mouth— probably to call him a jerk— but he grabbed the back of her neck and kissed her before she could say anything. She raked her fingernails down his spine, melting into the kiss.

Jericho slipped his hand between them again and brushed soft circles around her clit, working a needy whimper from her throat. And then he slid his middle finger into her tight core, rocking his wrist in deep, even strokes.

Marlee's cry of pleasure was muffled by their kissing. He felt her hold on him tighten as she started to shake.

When she finally shattered, her head fell back against the wall shouting a breathless, "Fuck—!"

By this time, Jericho was hard as a rock and dripping. His chest heaved against hers, holding her through every wave until she relaxed.

Their eyes danced, droplets of water gathering in his

eyelashes. Then Marlee was pushing him back, so she had room to get on her knees— giving him no time to react.

As her fingers wrapped around his length, Jericho inhaled sharply. He wondered if maybe teasing her so much had been a poorly thought-out plan because she always seemed to match his energy.

She looked up at him with those fiery amber eyes, her tan skin glistening as her hand caressed him.

Or the best idea I've ever had.

A little nervous but captivated by her, he watched as she brought him to her lips. His heart rate picked up, pressing his palms to the wall in an attempt to steady himself as she took the first inch slowly. Just the warmth of her mouth and the way her tongue swirled around the tip made him shudder.

Marlee worked him with her hand at the same time she sucked and rolled her tongue against the sensitive skin underneath.

He let out a hoarse groan, heat rushing over his body as he tried not to rock his hips forward. He felt like he was about to reach the peak and started to tense up.

But Marlee applied pressure at his base that staunched the rising of his release.

Her eyes met his for a moment, a little smirk playing on her lips.

Oh, fuck.

Then she pulled him back into her mouth, but deeper. And Jericho about lost his mind while she teased— only bringing him to the edge.

His jaw tightened, panting, and shaking.

"Dammit Marlee—" he growled, cutting off as her teeth just barely scraped under his head.

She tilted her head, taking her mouth away. Her hand stroked him slowly and firmly instead.

"You're such a—"

Her grip on his cock tightened, cutting him off again.

Her eyebrows lifted. "A what?"

"A tease," he rasped.

"I'm just finishing what you started," she purred as her hand moved faster— squeezed tighter.

The friction stole his words.

Marlee licked up his arousal.

And it was too much when she took him almost fully in her mouth.

With one stroke of her lips firmly locked around his cock he was undone. His muscles contracted, and he came in her mouth before he could try to pull away.

Jericho's lips parted letting out a guttural moan.

He was about to apologize, but she didn't pull away immediately— going slowly and sucking as she did.

He cursed under his breath as the sensation made his muscles jerk.

Running her thumb over her lips and chin, she tilted her head to look at him. Rendered speechless by her he just stared, trying to remember how to function.

"You good?" Marlee giggled softly, her freckled cheeks turning a pretty pink.

He laughed under his breath, also blushing as he brushed a curl away from her forehead.

"Better than good."

Jericho wrapped an arm across Marlee's torso as she leaned back against him. Resting his head against the wall behind where he sat on his bed, he sighed.

She tangled her fingers with his and ended the comfortable silence with a soft voice.

"Jerry?"

"Hm?"

"I wasn't drunk."

He lifted his pointer finger and wrapped it around hers.

Assuming she was talking about their first night together, he tilted his head to look at her.

"Yeah?"

It was all he said because he wanted her to tell him the truth but didn't want to speak for her.

"Yeah."

She looked up at him.

"I'm sorry I tried to use alcohol as my scapegoat. I think I was just freaking out."

"Freaking out about the production or sleeping with me?"

"Both," she sighed.

"It's not something I do— jumping into bed with people. And I don't think I realized that I actually liked you because I was too busy being frustrated with the production and all I needed to do, plus the pressure of the scout being at opening night." Marlee took a breath, her lashes lowering as she smiled a little. "Funny thing was that I couldn't tell the difference between being frustrated and stressed from how I felt about you."

He frowned.

"What do you mean?"

"You frustrate me."

She ran her fingers up his arm. "Because you were relaxed and so chill about the things I was uptight about. Because you made me want to let my guard down. And you were still nice to me after I acted like a bitch."

He smiled, pressing his lips to her head.

"I forgive you."

"Thanks," she laughed softly.

He pulled her closer, resting his chin on her shoulder.

"So, are you gonna tell me what you wrote in the binder?"

Her hand lifted to the side of his face. "I just added an extra 'to-do', to the list."

"Oh yeah?"

"Mhm."

"Did we check the box?"

She grinned.

"And some."

"So, did I get an A, or was that just extra credit, professor?"

"Let's just say you passed with flying colors," she giggled, patting the side of his face.

Jericho laughed against her shoulder.

"Oh—!"

Marlee started to move out of his arms, but his fingers pinched at her sides.

"Don't go away!"

She squirmed, trying to pry his fingers away as she snorted, "Stop— oh my god that tickles!" Marlee tried pushing his arms down, still laughing, "I'm just gonna get something, I'll be right back."

He raised an eyebrow.

"Promise?"

"Promise."

And she kept it as she walked back into the room, holding what looked like some folded clothes. He tilted his head as she handed them to him, and Jericho realized that they were the clothes she had run out of his dorm in.

He grinned at her.

"I thought for sure that you had thrown these away," he admitted, shifting the fabric in his hands.

She started to blush.

"I did. And then I dug them out and washed them, since, you know, you painted a masterpiece in that shirt."

"That was nice of you," he teased.

She shrugged with a half roll of her eyes and climbed over the bed into his lap. Hooking her arms around his neck she brushed a soft kiss over his lips.

Butterflies rushed through his body.

"Are you going to make me a grilled cheese, now?

"If the lady demands."

She smiled shyly.

"She does."

"One 'Jerry Special' coming up."

CHAPTER TWENTY-THREE

Marlee

"Is it done yet?"

"Can you let a man work?" Jericho laughed as he reached the spatula out to swat her backside. Despite his efforts to shoo her away, Marlee only came closer. She liked the way he teased her and they pushed each other's buttons.

"I'm hungry, Jerry," she whined, wrapping her arms around his torso.

He lifted his arm, resting it around her shoulders as he shook his head.

"You're so impatient."

She blinked up at him and lifted her hand to hold his that hung from her shoulder— intertwining their fingers.

"And? We've established this," she teased.

"Food is like art," he said, setting the spatula down and grabbing the handle of the pan. "It's only good if you take your time."

And then he shook the pan and flipped the grilled cheese.

She started to smile.

"Show off."

The corner of his mouth twitched up, but he didn't deny it. Watching him do his thing, Marlee started to get butterflies again.

He glanced at her.

"It's almost done."

Her shoulders lifted, her free hand brushing against his ribcage.

"Okay."

True to his word, the grilled cheese was done in a few minutes. He put it on a plate and slid it onto the counter in front of her. Taking half of the sandwich as he took the other, she held it up for cheers.

Jericho tapped his half against hers.

After one bite, Marlee paused and stared at him. That little worried line formed between his brows. A little more than impressed she took another bite and started to shake her head.

"Dude," she said around her food. "This is so good."

He just smiled.

Finishing the food, she picked up the plate and put it in the sink. And moved to hug Jericho from behind. She pressed her lips to his spine as her hands flattened over his heart. One of his lifted to cover hers.

"Thank you."

"You're welcome."

She kept hold of one of his hands as she took her arms away, pulling him back toward the bedroom. And she was happy that he didn't ask any questions as he followed, holding her hand. After Jericho shut the door behind them, Marlee climbed back onto the bed and tugged his hand so that he would join her.

Lifting his arm over her head, she laid back next to him so that her head rested on his bicep. She absently played with his fingers, looking over at him with a funny smile.

"How do you not have a girlfriend? You paint, dance, cook—you actually wash and fold your laundry."

"Apparently, I wasn't frustrating anyone enough."

She snorted, "Shut up. I'm serious."

He shrugged, pushing his hair away from his forehead.

"I don't really know." Jericho met her eyes, looking shy. "I hadn't met my person yet, I guess."

Marlee's heart did a little skipping dance in her chest,

rolling more to her side. His arm hugged her tighter around the backs of her shoulders.

"Are you saying I'm your person, Jericho?"

He started to smile, and up close she could see the blush tinting his cheekbones.

"I'm *asking*."

Marlee's brows lifted as she teased him, "Asking me what, Byers?"

He pulled her closer, his free hand pinching her side—making her laugh. But he flattened his palm, sliding it to her back instead of tickling her.

"I'm asking you to be my person— my girlfriend. The Elizabeth to my Darcy. The beast to my beauty."

"I think you got that the wrong way around, cowboy," she corrected, referring to his last statement.

But she smiled so much that it pulled out the dimple at one corner of her mouth.

"Only if you've had your coffee."

She smacked his shoulder with a little laugh, "Smartass."

He just smiled, his fingers starting a slow trail up and down her spine.

"One word, Marlee."

Smoothing her hand over his shoulder to his neck, she brushed her thumb along his jaw.

"Yes."

"Yeah?"

"Yeah."

She pulled him in for a soft kiss and Jericho pressed his palm into her lower back, drawing it out. Little dancing sparks rolled along her spine as she pushed her fingers up into the back of his hair.

Unlike their earlier kisses that were almost frenzied, this was more of a slow dance. And Marlee was content to take her time. Jericho seemed on the same page, tilting his head this way and that.

Marlee paused, eyes closed.

Their breath mingled.

"You're my boyfriend," she mused, out of breath.

"Didn't see that coming, did you?" he teased quietly.

She smiled.

"I really didn't," she told him, placing another light kiss on the corner of his mouth.

His hand moved up to the back of her neck, turning into her kiss. She blushed, starting to feel that tingling sensation between her legs.

He really is something else...

"Are you happy?" he whispered, their lips brushing.

"Most ardently," she giggled quietly.

He pulled her back in, their dance of kisses picking up again. Marlee's head started to spin when Jericho gave her bottom lip a gentle tug with his teeth. She shifted closer, his leg moving between hers as she hooked one over his hip.

And the slow, sweet kisses turned deep and breathless.

When he rubbed his thigh against her core, she hummed against his kiss. Bringing her hand down his neck and torso, she wedged it between them until she found what she was searching for. This time he didn't stop her when her palm brushed back and forth over his erection.

Dipping her chin away from his lips, she looked up into his sea-green eyes. The more she stroked him the tighter he held her.

Marlee loved it.

"Ready for another round, Byers?"

"Hell yeah."

Sitting up, he helped her out of his shirt. She undid the waistband tie of his sweatpants. And then she grabbed the condom from his bedside table. He gave her a confused look.

She tapped it against his chest.

"Brought one in after the shower, just in case."

She winked.

He grinned, opening it. But handed it back to her.

"Since you're better at it than I am," he teased.

Laughing under her breath she took it and wrapped him up.

Seeing the fire in his eyes, she pulled him in for a kiss.

He tugged her hair back, kissing her mouth, and moved his lips down her neck as he backed her to the bed. But instead of laying her back, he turned her around and pulled her body up against his.

A soft sound of surprise escaped her as his hands went in opposite directions. One caressed her breasts while the other teased between her legs. Marlee leaned her head back against the front of his shoulder, grabbing one of his forearms to steady herself.

God, he's so good at this.

His voice was rough against her ear, "Bend over."

But he didn't wait for her to do as he asked.

Instead, he used one hand— pushing it up her spine to fold her over the bed while the other held her hip. The heartbeat between her legs intensified. She loved when he got bossy. And the way his hands fit perfectly around her hips.

As his hands squeezed her tight, she felt his cock rub against her aching center. Dropping her lower back, she pushed her backside against him and groaned.

He pushed forward, notching himself against her. And then he grabbed her hips again. In a smooth motion, he sheathed himself inside her.

Still sore from all of their earlier activities, the pressure made her gasp.

"You feel so good," he moaned— the compliment had her throbbing around him.

When he moved inside her she couldn't even speak, each thrust only working whimpering cries from her throat.

His hand let go of her hip, picking up her ponytail instead. The way he tugged at it sent a shiver down her spine. She felt him wrap it around his hand and she knew that she was about to get all the attitude she had ever shown him fucked right out of her.

CHAPTER TWENTY-FOUR

Jericho

"Sanjay, wait, I have a better serving plate than that for the cookies!"

Jericho had watched Marlee boss Sanjay around for about ten minutes, thoroughly amused. It had started with how the booze would be stored and displayed to keep it cool. The cans and bottles were nicely arranged in an ice cooler now after Sanjay had given up trying to appease her.

It was fun to watch her with her friends.

"This plate is fine—" Sanjay started to argue, but Marlee set the serving plate down next to the plate currently holding the cookies.

She looked at her friend and he sighed, "Okay, at least if they are on that, they won't fall off when August grabs one with his meaty paws."

Ada ducked under Sanjay's arm, stealing a cookie before scurrying off.

"Thanks, Sanny!"

"Hey—! You can't just eat those! They are special! I don't care if you're the birthday girl Ada Varner, it's rude to enjoy your birthday cookies before I sing to you," he called after her in a teasing voice that got louder the further, she went.

Her muffled laughter sounded down the hall and Sanjay started to grin— blowing out a breath that made his raven curls jump on his forehead.

Marlee started arranging the cookies on the new platter and Jericho laughed with a shake of his head when Sanjay looked at him with wide, 'help me' eyes.

When she was done, Marlee fluffed Sanjay's hair.

"Thanks for making the cookies, Sanny."

"You're welcome," he sighed, laughing.

He appraised the spread of snacks and drinks. Then he stared past Jericho into the small living space of the dorm. He held up a finger like he was remembering something. Then he turned and followed where Ada had gone down the hall.

"Ada, where did you store the karaoke machine?"

Marlee came over then, typing something on her phone. She stood between his legs, tapping the screen one last time before sitting on his thigh. When she wrapped an arm around his shoulders, Jericho's arm slipped around her back.

She set her phone down and smiled at him.

"Hey, cowboy."

He kissed her shoulder.

"Hey."

And then he frowned. "What's this I hear about karaoke?"

He wasn't sure he could stomach that. Maybe if it were just him, Marlee, and August, but he was still getting to know the others.

"We can't have a party without the karaoke and August's loud singing," she told him.

Jericho's brows rose.

"I bet we could."

Marlee laughed.

"You don't like karaoke?"

"Not particularly."

"Party pooper."

Jericho pinched her side with his fingers, making her squirm.

"I'm sure August and Ada will love to take the spotlight anyways. I can just watch."

"No." She pried his fingers away, trying to hold them away from her.

He smiled, wrestling a little with her as he tried to poke her.

"Stop—" she laughed. "C'mon, I'll sing with you, it will be fun!"

He eyed her, not convinced that would make him feel better. But it was sweet of her to offer.

"Maybe," was all he said.

There was a knock on the door, and by the sound of the loud laughter, August was here— with friends.

"Sanjay, the door!" Marlee shouted.

"I'm busy, woman!" Sanjay yelled back.

Another knock.

"Is it unlocked?" Jericho asked when Marlee didn't move off his lap.

She shrugged.

"I don't know."

"You're not gonna get the door?"

"I'm comfortable," she said, the backs of her nails brushing up his neck and back down.

One corner of his mouth lifted in a lopsided smile.

"You can come back. I'm not going anywhere."

She made a pouty face but relented and as she stood, he slapped her ass. And it was, of course, at this moment that Sanjay and Ada decided to reappear.

"Jerry, I didn't need to see that!" Sanjay snorted, covering his eyes.

Ada's nose scrunched— grinning. She high-fived Marlee as she walked past, who giggled and went to answer the door.

Jericho's neck heated but he laughed.

It had only been a week since he and Marlee had made things official, but they still couldn't seem to get enough of each other. August had been equal parts mortified and over the moon, two of his best friends were falling for each other. Ada had threatened violence to his nether regions if he hurt her best friend and Sanjay had hugged him.

He hadn't expected any less from Marlee's friends, who were now also his he realized.

August came through the door, followed by another guy Jericho didn't recognize as Sanjay started setting up the karaoke machine. Marlee hugged August who rubbed his fist on top of her head with a grin, then she moved to the other dude to give him a side hug.

Jericho tried to act like he wasn't watching when she pointed him out— the guy's gaze shifting toward where she pointed.

"Happy birthday, Ada!" August boomed, hugging her tight enough to lift her feet off the ground.

Her laugh was strangled as she hugged him back, thanking him for saying so.

Sanjay's eyes bounced between all the people in the room and then to Jericho.

"I might need help. This thing does not cooperate."

"Okay, I don't know how much help I will be."

"You've got experience with handling Marlee, you're good," he teased, lightly punching Jericho's shoulder and handing him some of the aux cords.

He looked back at his girlfriend, grinning.

"Right."

Untangling some of the cords he helped Sanjay set up the karaoke. He almost asked who the guy Marlee was talking to was, but he figured she would introduce them.

"Hey! Hands off the cookies!" Sanjay yelled at August who had already spotted them. "We sing the song first, guys. That's the rule."

His words were met with exaggerated groans.

Jericho shook his head.

"You're almost as bossy as Marlee."

Sanjay didn't even miss a beat as he plugged in the last of the cords, fixing Jericho with a comically sassy look.

"I could probably out boss her if I wanted to."

"Oh yeah? I'd like to see that," he laughed.

"Jerry, stop flirting with me, she's right over there."

Jericho snorted.

Picking up a pillow as he stood up and then smacked it against his friend's face as he walked away. Marlee wove around her friends toward him with the new guy in tow.

She glanced at Sanjay who was snickering to himself.

"Do I want to know?"

"No," Jericho laughed.

She grinned, giving Sanjay a light shove on the shoulder as he passed her.

Sanjay held out a hand to the guy and they proceeded to do some kind of intricate handshake.

"Jericho, this is Ada's brother, Adler. Adler this is my boyfriend, Jericho," she introduced, looking happy as her cheeks brightened in color.

"Hey, nice to meet you," Jericho greeted, holding out a hand.

Adler shook his hand and then fist-bumped him.

"You too, man."

August came over and hugged Jericho, keeping an arm around him as he pointed at Sanjay.

"Sing the birthday ballad so we can eat the damn cookies, Sanny."

"Why am I always the one?" Sanjay asked with a laugh.

"You're the only one with a decent voice. We don't want the glasses to shatter if August tries to hit any highnotes," Adler said, grinning.

"Or any notes, for that matter," Ada snorted, grinning at her friend.

August nodded like he hadn't just been roasted.

Sanjay shook his head.

"I happen to know Marlee Firth-Diaz also can sing."

Jericho looked at her, gasping dramatically at the same time August did.

She waved a hand.

"I'm not doing this by myself. You wouldn't disappoint your best friends, would you?" Sanjay crossed his arms, fixing her with a smug look.

"Fine," she sighed with a smile, going to hook an arm around Sanjay's back.

He hugged his arm around her shoulders as he began to sing a very odd version of the birthday song, but thoroughly impressing Jericho with his clear tenor.

Marlee joined in with Sanjay, harmonizing with him in a rich alto. August let go of Jericho and clapped his hands. And the rest of them joined the song, ending with a loud cheer as Ada hooked her arms around Marlee and Sanjay's necks, smiling.

"Can we have cookies now?" she asked, laughing.

Sanjay let go of Marlee as she moved away, turning Ada to the plate of his famous cookies.

"You can. Everyone else can wait."

The group milled around the small kitchen, grabbing snacks and drinks as they laughed and talked. Marlee brought Jericho a Guinness, pulling one of his arms over her shoulder and resting her back against him.

August was first to the karaoke machine, performing a very animated version of 'Never Gonna Give You Up'. Ada almost choked on her cookie when he started shaking his ass.

By the time Sanjay got up to take a turn and sang a moving version of 'My Heart Will Go On', everyone had so much to drink that August might have cried and somehow Jericho ended up with Marlee sitting on his lap and then Ada on top of her.

The girls were giggling so much as they tried to sing along that Jericho finally shoved them off. They fell onto the couch, reaching and hugging each other as they sang and laughed.

He laughed, shaking his head as he realized that, if not for August, he would have never gotten here. Probably wouldn't have stuck around so many extroverts if anything. But he kind of liked it.

And now, he even had a fellow introvert, Adler, sitting next to him and sharing looks, watching the chaos. But mostly, Jericho watched Marlee and the way she lit up around these people that she loved.

It was his favorite part of the night.

CHAPTER TWENTY-FIVE

Marlee

"Rock, paper, scissors for dinner," Ada challenged, placing her fist on her open palm.

Marlee turned to her friend sitting in the passenger seat of her car, placing her own fist in her palm.

"Let's go. Best of three or just one round— cutthroat?"

"One and done," she smirked and started counting. "One... two . . . three— shoot!"

Marlee landed on scissors and Ada on paper.

"Dammit," her friend muttered.

"Sushi."

"I knew you would pick that. But hey, I'm not mad about it. If I eat any more steak or potatoes I might barf," she complained.

"August on a protein trip again?"

Marlee turned on her car and started to pull out of the mall parking lot. She eyed Ada, wondering if there was more happening between her friends than just hanging out or surfing.

She nodded, pulling her blonde curls into a messy bun and rolling down her window.

"Yeah— god it's hot outside today."

Deciding to broach the subject, since Ada didn't give much up, Marlee tried to sound only mildly curious.

So, you guys have been hanging out a lot."

There was a pause that she tried not to read into. She didn't have a problem with her friends dating, but it almost felt like they weren't being honest with her.

Or maybe they don't even know what's going on between them. Been there.

"He's fun, and helping me with my workout routine."

"Mhm."

"And we both like that new reality show, so we watch that together."

"That's cool," she commented, her voice rising in pitch.

She felt Ada looking at her.

"Something you wanna say?"

"No, just curious."

But Marlee couldn't help herself.

"I mean, you guys stay out way later than the gym is even open," she added.

Ada snorted, "Why are you being so weird about this? You're acting like a dad or something."

Marlee turned into the parking lot of the sushi restaurant, parked, and then looked at Ada.

"Sorry— I'm just making sure you're okay."

She looked confused. "Why wouldn't I be? It's Auggie."

"You know I love you both, right?"

"Yes?" Ada said slowly.

"Okay, then you will know that I just want you both happy."

"Right…"

Marlee tucked her hair behind her ears.

"So, if you guys are more than friends that's cool. But just be careful, okay?"

What she wanted to say was that she didn't think August was ready for a serious relationship. The guy had a different date every few weeks. Marlee didn't think he was a player, just that he was irresponsible when it came to girls.

And she didn't want Ada to get hurt because of that.

Ada was visibly blushing and looked about two seconds from spilling her guts.

Marlee waited.

Her friend blew out a breath, "I don't know what he and I are, Mar. Honestly."

"Did you not want to tell me what was going on?"

"It wasn't that I didn't want to. You've just been busy with Jericho."

Suddenly she felt like a shit friend.

She had been gone a lot. A lot of the time it was overnight too. And she hadn't paid attention to how being so wrapped up in her boyfriend had affected her best friend.

"I'm sorry. He's distracting as fuck."

Ada smiled.

"Yeah because you guys can't *stop* fucking," Ada laughed, poking her arm.

"That's not all we do," Marlee denied, blushing madly.

"Hey, I'm not dissing it. I wish I had that," she said and reached for her friend's hand. "I'm happy for you, really. But I miss you."

"I miss you too and I'm glad today worked out."

Ada nodded.

"Let's go get some sushi, girl."

"You won't hear me argue," Marlee replied.

Ada's brows lifted.

"That's a first."

She laughed, "Shut up."

They exited the car.

And as they moved around it, Marlee hooked her arm through Ada's. For once, she wasn't worrying and obsessing over the production and it felt great to be present in the moment with her best friend.

◆ ◆ ◆

After a few more stores, Marlee had two bags in her hands. She had been shopping for an outfit for the upcoming dress rehearsal and for opening night. And was happy with what she picked out.

Ada found a few things as well.

And as they came out of the elevator on their floor she caught sight of the broad shoulders she had come to recognize from across a room.

Jericho pushed off the wall, waving a hand at her and Ada. She was going to hug him, but he took her bags from her instead.

"Uh, hey?" she laughed as he pressed a kiss to her temple.

"Hey."

Ada started to smile a little maniacally.

"What's up, Jerebear?"

He blinked, his eyebrows quirking funnily.

"Jerebear?" he repeated, glancing at Marlee.

"Your new nickname," she clarified.

Ada nodded.

Marlee almost laughed at the look on his face, like he was trying to process that but just gave up and accepted it. She wrapped her arms around his torso as Ada unlocked their door.

"What brings you to my side of town, cowboy?"

"You forgot something," he said quietly, slipping a folded lacy thing into the front pocket of her jeans.

Heat bloomed across her cheekbones. She knew exactly what she had forgotten at his place the last time she had been there.

"Thank you," she laughed under her breath.

Jericho glanced at Ada and the now-open door. "Mind if I come in for a minute?"

"Sure," she said, giving Marlee a suggestive look.

Moving inside their dorm, Jericho set Marlee's bags on the counter. Ada pulled out an Arizona tea and grabbed a cookie.

"Peace, dudes, I got homework."

And she left them alone. Marlee bit back a smile knowing full well that her friend had finished said homework at the start of the weekend and that she would probably be talking to August.

"So, what's up? I didn't think I would see you until class on

Monday."

He shrugged, teasing her, "Couldn't wait that long for you to boss me around again."

With a roll of her eyes, Marlee slipped her arms around his neck.

"Well, I missed your smart mouth anyways." She kissed him once. "Wanna stay for a movie and dessert?"

"Is Ada okay with that?"

"She'll be fine. I think she might be hanging out with August tonight, and if not she can watch the movie with us."

"Cool."

"Cool cool cool," she giggled. "You want anything to drink?"

"Nah, I'm good."

"Okay."

Marlee pulled him toward the couch, dropping her purse next to the TV stand. Jericho grabbed the remote from the coffee table and sat down. She moved a pillow to his lap, lying down on him with a sigh.

"Why do humans have to wear shoes," she grumbled, kicking her boots off and tossing them over the back of the couch.

Jericho laughed under his breath, his fingers trailing through the ends of her hair.

"Blisters?"

She nodded.

"I'm sorry," he offered and Marlee shrugged, smiling.

"What should we watch?"

Jericho looked at the TV and then at her, setting the remote down on the arm of the couch.

"I'd rather just talk to you."

Marlee studied him. He looked tired, and she started to wonder if she was taking up too much of his time lately. Pulling his arm over her torso, she brushed her fingers over his skin.

"What's up?"

His eyes moved to where his fingers wrapped and ran

through her hair. As she spent more time with him she was beginning to understand that his hesitating was not because he didn't want to answer her, or talk. More often, he only needed a minute to gather his thoughts. She just needed to be patient.

So she waited for him to speak, even though the loaded silence was grating on her.

"I've just felt a little burnt out with my art."

She frowned.

"Oh?"

Her fingers stilled, flattening her palm over his forearm.

"Too much work on the set design sapping your creativity?"

"Well, there's that, but I think I've been so busy that I don't have the time to paint. And even when I do I'm tired from the internship..."

Her thumb moved in a semi-circle, feeling responsible for how he felt.

She started to ask in a slow, gentle tone, "And from spending too much time with me?"

He met her eyes.

"I'd rather spend time with you than at the internship but I need the hours of experience if I want a job after this."

"I know, but I don't want to take away time from something that is important to you," she told him.

A smile lifted one corner of his mouth.

"You've helped me to slow down, but I don't want to be *what* slows *you* down, Jerry."

"You're not, I just suck at managing my time," he sighed, tugging softly at her hair. "Besides, you're important too."

She squeezed his arm, all kinds of butterflies stirring inside of her.

"Well . . . you're lucky that you have a control freak for a girlfriend. I can help with the schedule thing."

He made a face and she laughed, "I'll just help you make a little calendar."

"I guess it couldn't hurt."

She started to grin, a little too excited to start working

on a personalized calendar for him. He looked like he was unsure if he would regret this. Marlee tapped his arm, suddenly remembering something.

"I just had an idea."

Jericho still looked wary, like she would suggest staying with him and being his personal alarm clock or something.

Over the top, even for me. But still fun to think about, she mused.

"You should apply to a gallery— debut some of your work there!"

"That sounds like more work is being added to my schedule."

"How long have you been at the tattoo shop?"

"I don't know, probably since school started last year?"

"More than six months?" she asked.

He nodded.

"Yeah."

"Quit."

"Huh? I can't just quit, Marlee."

"Six months seems like a good amount of time. And they aren't paying you, so if you quit and did the gallery instead it would diversify your resume."

"Portfolio."

"Right, portfolio."

She watched him contemplate this. He didn't immediately shoot down the idea, so she hoped it would give him some ideas about improving his situation.

"Just ideas. I don't want to tell you what to do, but I want to help."

And she meant it. She and her friends and even Jericho often joked about her being bossy or controlling— which she owned up to— but truly, she just wanted to help him.

"I'll think about it," he said, staring across the room.

"Okay."

She smiled, glancing at the TV.

"Wanna watch our movie?"

That made him grin.

"I don't think I could ever say no to Pride and Prejudice."

"You've got the remote."

He turned on the TV, playfully shoving her so she was half falling off him and the couch.

"Better go grab some cookies and tissues before I start this without you."

Marlee let out a screaming sort of laugh and tried to get her legs underneath herself.

"If you do, I'm not gonna share the cookies," she threatened, trying to crawl over his legs as he tried to block her from getting out of the living room.

Shoving his feet down, her hands shot out to grab the pillow still on his lap and started whacking him with it.

He laughed, grabbing the pillow with his much larger hand, and yanked it away from her. Immediately, she tried to run for the kitchen, but he still landed one hit on her backside.

With a wide grin and lights in his eyes, he teased her, "Don't start what you can't finish."

"I think we both know I am very capable in that regard, Byers. But, fuck around and find out."

She smirked.

"Bring me a cookie and I just might."

"Deal."

CHAPTER TWENTY-SIX

Jericho

The days were flying by leading up to the dress rehearsal and Jericho was glad that most of the hard work for the set was over. Now it was just touch-ups and tweaks. The problem was that he didn't have much to do besides watch Marlee direct everyone.

And more times than not, it just straight-up turned him on.

Lena wiped her pink hair off her forehead, glancing at him and then at Marlee.

She grinned.

"Hey, lover boy, help me carry this stuff backstage would ya?"

"Sure," he agreed, smiling.

He picked up one end of the stack of boards they were going to be using as bearings and supports for the larger set pieces. Lena grabbed the other and they carried them to the back where the stage crew thanked them and began sorting things.

"It's a full-blown hive in here today," Jericho commented, watching all the crew members working together, the actors rehearsing or going over their script and getting fitted for last-minute costume details.

Lena nodded.

"And I don't think we have anything left to do before rehearsal tomorrow."

She held up a hand and Jericho high-fived it.

"I can't believe that's tomorrow."

"Time flies when you're having fun, or in your case, arguing and getting stuck in closets with the director," she snickered.

Jericho started to grin.

"Exactly— having fun."

"Speaking of, here comes the boss now."

He looked to where Lena pointed with a jerk of her chin. Sure enough, Marlee was headed his way, binder in hand. He kept his face trained as it was kind of their thing to pretend, they still disliked each other in front of the theater crew and cast.

Lena threw up a peace sign and headed back into the auditorium.

"Need something?" Jericho crossed his arms.

Marlee's amber eyes flicked over him.

"Step into my office, Byers."

Not waiting for him to respond, she turned and headed away from the auditorium. Jericho followed, unsure where she was taking him. And after they rounded a corner, Marlee opened a door that, if he had to guess, was a small dressing room.

Pausing, he raised an eyebrow at her and Marlee glanced behind them. It must have been all clear because she grabbed his shirtfront and pulled him inside after her.

Jericho's hand fumbled for the door, trying to carefully shut it as she reached up to his neck and pulled him down for a kiss. He was trying not to grin so much as she kissed him but then she was giggling against his mouth.

"Shhhh!" she shushed him.

Burying his fingers in her hair, he kissed her harder even as they both laughed from somewhere deep in their chests.

Marlee pushed him back against the door, letting go of his shirt and instead slipping her fingers under its hem. Her palm warmed the skin over his beating heart.

Pulling back, Jericho brushed her cheeks with his thumbs.

"Get what you needed?"

"Yes, but also...not even close," she whispered, pressing her body against his. His hands moved down, fingers kneading the back of her neck. And hers tugged at the back of his hair.

"We still on for tonight?" he asked, trying not to think too much about the way her soft curves always fit so well against him.

Marlee had helped him come up with a calendar to help manage his time and so far it was helping him get more rest. They had also decided to only plan for one date a week. Not that they kept to that. He already had a space in one of his drawers that was hers for when she stayed over because they couldn't keep away.

Her chin dipped in a nod.

"Yeah, are you picking me up? Or should I just come over?"

"Meet me in the art studio. I'm going over there right after this," he told her, and her eyes lit up.

"I can walk over with you. If you don't mind waiting while I give the group the run-down about the dress rehearsal?"

"I think I can do that," he said, smiling.

She smiled back, bringing his mouth back to hers. Jericho's fingers found the collar of her button-up blouse, tracing the edge down to the first button at her chest.

Her fingers slipped down the line of his stomach.

With a twist of his fingers, he undid the button and smoothed his hand under the fabric and over her skin. Marlee hooked her fingers in his waistband, running the backs of her nails against his hip.

Before he could undo another button on her blouse, she dipped her chin to break the kiss.

"Woah there, cowboy," she breathed with a smirk, pulling her fingers from his waistband.

But her lashes lowered as she palmed his hard-on.

Jericho's breathing hitched.

"Can't get too riled up in here."

"Dammit Marlee," he half-laughed and half-growled.

She stepped away, fixing her shirt.

"You can punish me later," she teased.

"As always, I will enjoy the fuck out of it," he told her. But he had his own plans for the night, and since she liked a good game of teasing, Jericho would give her a run for her money.

◆ ◆ ◆

Marlee looked at the pile of pillows set by one of the windows of the studio.

"You want me to sit here?"

"Yes."

She raised an eyebrow.

Jericho laughed gently, "Please? You can still work in your binder."

"Are you going to draw me?"

"Sit."

"Okay, mister bossy," she snorted, sitting on the pillows.

She opened the binder and clicked her pen a few times. Jericho started to prep his canvas, ignoring Marlee's glances on purpose.

"I applied to the gallery," he told her, keeping his eyes on the canvas as he brushed varying watercolors over it.

Her voice lilted, "You did?"

"I did."

He rinsed the brush and started blending colors.

"I actually applied the night after you suggested it."

There was a pause and so Jericho looked over at her. He couldn't tell what she was thinking even though she was smiling.

"Wow, that's exciting. Have you heard back?"

"Yeah, they really liked my portfolio and offered to feature me as a local artist for their next open house."

When he had gotten the response to his application, Jericho had been shocked. It was an odd thing to be an artist— to both be so in love with your art and also, in some moments, be utterly disgusted with it. His friends and family all loved the pieces and projects they had seen, but it was still hard for him to believe that he was good enough.

"Of course, they did," she gloated with a grin.

He smiled, blushing a little at her confidence in him.

"So, will you quit the internship then?"

He shrugged, going back to his canvas.

"Maybe, if the gallery goes well."

"That's probably smart," she commented. "But I don't see how it could go wrong for you, Jerry."

"Things can always go sideways. I don't think I can even let myself think that this will open up big doors for me until it actually does, because if it doesn't work out, it could suck the life out of my art for a while," he admitted. "I can't afford that."

Marlee set down her binder, closing it. He felt her studying him.

"Well, I think you're talented and that you have what it takes to do whatever you dream of."

She's adorable.

He couldn't bring himself to look at her, sure that he would ditch the canvas for her immediately if he did.

"Talent only gets you so far. Unfortunately, I'm not super great at the people thing— or networking," he confessed.

"I can help with that. I'll be right next to you the whole time," she assured him.

Jericho couldn't help but smile as he blotted at the bright, happy oranges and yellows with his brush.

"Yeah?"

"Yeah."

Marlee opened her binder again, leaning against the pillows as they fell into a comfortable silence. For an hour, Jericho worked on his canvas, and she wrote down notes— probably using an entire block of her mini sticky notes.

He paused, studying the soft curves of her face that were lit by the evening light outside. Her tan skin looked golden, framed by the soft, tawny brown of her hair. He wasn't sure he could capture all the things she was on a canvas.

Setting her pen down, her eyes lifted to meet his. Marlee

tilted her head, some of her hair tumbling over her shoulder. He didn't hide the way his eyes roamed over every part of her. She set the binder aside as their eyes continued to have an unspoken conversation.

Jericho put his brush in the water cup, wiping his hands down the front of his jeans. Their gazes caressed and danced over each other— touching without closing the distance.

"We should get out of here," she suggested quietly and pulled her hair over her shoulder. Her eyes warmed him from across the room.

He picked the brush back up and tapped it against the canvas.

"I'm not done."

"Oh?"

She sounded impatient.

One corner of his mouth twitched.

"The canvas needs . . . something."

"Inspiration?"

Jericho's eyes were drawn to her at the sultry tone of her voice.

He watched unabashedly as she started to take down the buttons of her shirt, one side slipping slowly off of her shoulder.

He almost forgot that *he* was supposed to be stringing *her* out.

So, he dipped his brush in paint and went to work.

"Color me, inspired."

CHAPTER TWENTY-SEVEN

Marlee

Marlee adjusted her glasses, sitting back in the theater chair. The day had been chaotic, to say the least. Waking up before her alarms and drinking not one but two coffees had done nothing to help her nerves. If anything, it only made things worse.

But she was here now, halfway through dress rehearsal, and things were going much smoother than anticipated.

She tapped her pen against her notes for the cast, which was a lot shorter than she would like. Having fewer things to work on almost made her more nervous than if she had been disappointed in their performance.

That's stupid, I should be proud. Focus on the positives.

By the end of the rehearsal, she was tearing up. Bennet and Talia's performance of the last scenes was moving, and she was confident that the scout would be blown away.

As the curtains closed, Marlee stood and clapped her hands — even giving a whistle. The tech crew followed her lead from where they sat in the sound booth. Making her way down the aisle and up to the stage to meet her cast and crew she kept clapping.

"Guys, that was amazing!"

There was a round of 'thank yous' and smiles and high-fives.

She glanced at her watch.

About thirty minutes over time.

"Okay, good work, I will send notes to Mr. Emery and you should see an email from him about those notes. I'll see you all next weekend for the big night!"

There was no slow exit this time as everyone left in groups, talking excitedly. Bennet and Talia paused as they passed Marlee.

"Hey, boss, you coming out for drinks?" Bennet asked, grinning.

"No, thanks. I've got other plans."

And, as if on cue, she spotted Jericho come into the auditorium.

Her smile grew.

"Speak of the devil— catch you guys later."

Talia grinned. "Bye Marlee!"

"Bye!" she called to them over her shoulder.

Jericho reached out his hand for her as she approached. Marlee slipped her fingers against his palm.

"Well, hello," he drawled.

"Hey— oh!" Marlee's returned greeting turned into a surprised giggle as he lifted her hand to give her a gentle spin.

Seeing how his eyes took in her outfit, she remembered that she had dressed up not just for the rehearsal but for dinner out. Her cheeks turned pink at his obvious approval of the black dress with flowy fabric that hugged her hips and flared softly to her ankles.

Lifting up one of her strappy heels, she smiled.

"You like?"

"Very much," he said with a grin.

She looked him over in his nice dress shirt and pants. She reached up and tugged on the leather necktie.

"I like too, very Texas-chic, cowboy," she teased.

"Yeah, thought it was a nice touch. Left my boots at home, though. Thought it would be too much for you."

"You have cowboy boots," she marveled.

The thought of him in wranglers and a white tee with his

hat and boots was a little too much for her brain to handle.

Her blush deepened.

"Of course."

He was grinning like he knew exactly how that little fact affected her. Marlee just giggled as they started out the doors.

She swung their hands, the cool evening air playing with the ends of her hair.

"What's for dinner, Jerry?"

"I have a place in mind."

"Always so mysterious," she sighed, smiling.

He pulled at her hand and brought her to his side, wrapping his arm around her shoulders.

"I thought that's what you liked about me?"

"Among other things."

He opened the passenger door for her and as she got in the truck, Marlee kissed his cheek.

She laughed when he swatted her backside.

On the road, Marlee was about to pester him again for the name of the restaurant he was taking her to, but her phone started to ring. Jericho glanced over, one eyebrow quirking. Marlee checked the caller ID and immediately answered.

She looked at Jericho and spoke into the phone, "Hey, mom!"

He smiled.

"Marlee, *mi bonita!*"

The sweet lilt of her mother's voice made her grin.

"*¿Cómo estás?*"

"*Muy buena*— Very good."

"Mama, I'm gonna put you on speaker so you can say hi to Jerry."

"Oh, *sí!*"

Marlee tapped the speaker button and held the phone up between her and Jericho.

Before she could affirm to her mom that she was on speaker phone, Jericho leaned in saying, "¡Hola!"

Her mom made an impressed, 'oooh' at his mediocre Spanish.

Marlee covered her laugh with her hand.

"¡*Hola* Jerry! Marlee has told me a lot about you."

"Hopefully lots of good things," he laughed, glancing at Marlee.

"Oh— *sí, sí*. All good things."

Jericho shared a look with Marlee like he didn't fully believe that, and she shrugged.

"So, what's up? You never call me this late, mama."

"Would you be able to come home for the weekend? Gi-Gi got into trouble and won't talk to me."

Marlee frowned, suddenly worried.

"Is she okay?"

"She's fine. I think she just needs someone to talk some sense into her. Since she started dating that boy, she's just not herself."

Now she was really worried. Taking her mom off the speaker, she pressed the phone to her ear and tugged at the ends of her curls.

"What happened?" she asked as Jericho pulled into the parking lot of a very nice-looking steakhouse.

"They got caught trespassing or something— like I said she won't talk to me."

Marlee sighed, glancing at Jericho who turned off his truck.

With a worried look in his eyes, he tilted his head.

She made a face, probably full of too many emotions.

"Yeah, I can drive home in the morning."

"Why don't you just fly?"

"Because plane tickets are expensive, mama," she laughed.

"I have frequent flyer points, you use those," she demanded, which only made Marlee smile more.

"Okay, sure. Send me the ticket, but don't book the flight for earlier than five in the morning, please."

"Sure, *mi bonita.*"

"Alright, see you tomorrow, mama."

"*Te amo*, Marlee."

"*Te amo*," she repeated, making a kissing noise into the phone before hanging up.

Jericho shifted his keys in his hands as she put her phone away and sighed.

"Everything okay?" he asked.

"I don't know. Sounds like G-money is in trouble and dating a loser. She won't talk to my mom."

She looked at the restaurant.

"This looks nice."

He looked over and nodded.

"It had good reviews." Then he frowned as his eyes found hers again. "I hope she's okay."

"Me too."

She hooked her purse strap over her shoulder and sighed, "Let's go eat."

Inside was exactly what Marlee expected from a steakhouse, with a ranch-style interior and plush booth seating. The hostess sat them near the fireplace that sat in the middle of the dining area. As Jericho pushed her seat in for her, she thanked him and set her purse at her feet.

It took her a minute to decide what she wanted, but he laid his menu flat after a quick glance. The first few times they had gone out to dinner, they had talked so much and Marlee hadn't been ready to order so many times in a row that the waiter had been visibly irked. And, as a result, she had been annoyed by her own indecisiveness.

It was now their rule to decide on food first and then talk, so Jericho patiently waited for her to decide and sipped on the water glass that their waitress had already dropped off.

Deciding on the New York strip steak, she lowered the menu— accidentally slapping it against the table very loudly.

She snorted when Jericho flinched. His eyes widened and he shook his head.

"Tell me how you really feel," he teased.

She rolled her eyes, adjusting the menus so they were stacked nicely. Normally, she would have teased him back, but she was still worrying about what kind of trouble Gianna had really got herself into. Jericho's hands reached over and covered hers, running his thumbs over her knuckles.

"You, okay?"

"I'm just worried."

He nodded.

Marlee thought for a moment and perked up at the idea she had. "Do you wanna come with me?"

"Back home?"

"Yeah." She didn't know why she was blushing so much at this question.

One corner of his mouth lifted as he squeezed her hands.

"I would, but the Gallery debut is on Monday, and I think I still need to touch up some of my pieces."

"Oh, right."

She hadn't forgotten about the gallery per se, it just hadn't been at the front of her mind.

He looked at their hands.

"Will you be able to make it back for it?"

"Of course," she agreed immediately. "I don't want to miss that."

"Okay, cool. I just don't think I could do it without you there," he told her, looking unsure of himself.

She squeezed his hands back. "You could. But I want to be there."

He smiled at her.

"Are you nervous?"

"Very much," he laughed lightly.

She was about to reassure him— tell him that she was also a wreck thinking about opening night for Beauty and The Beast, but the waitress came back. And after she took their order, Jericho and Marlee started talking about other things. And instead of spending the night, she asked him to drop her off at home so she could pack because her mom sent her the ticket.

And much to her dismay, it was scheduled for tomorrow at four in the morning.

CHAPTER TWENTY-EIGHT

Jericho

The morning of the gallery debut, Jericho had gotten up ready to take on the day and had walked across campus to the studio so he could make sure everything was in place.

Originally, he had planned for Marlee to be here so they could get coffee together and round up the three pieces he had selected for the gallery. Other than missing her, he felt that it might have been better this way considering the highlight piece he had was for her and he didn't want her to see it until it was hanging under the studio lights.

It was still too early to go and set up, so Jericho went to work inspecting every canvas for any needed touch-ups or tweaks. But he was happy with his work so, instead, he picked up another project and tried to distract himself by passing the time.

He didn't have to wait for long before his phone went off.

Pulling it out of his pocket he checked his notifications.

There were two new messages from 'The Professor'.

He grinned.

Marlee: Morning cowboy

Marlee: you better be up lol

Jericho: howdy.

Jericho: i've been up since the crack of dawn. proud of me? ;)

Marlee: wow look at you ;)

He smiled, setting down the brush he was using.

Jericho: is your sister ok? <3

Marlee: she's fine, i just talked to her again, and I'm already wishing she would dump this loser.

He frowned, resting his head back against the wall. This kid had to be something else for Marlee and her family to be so against him.

Jericho: really? Is he that bad?

Marlee: he's a deadbeat. a guitarist in this garage band that's going "only three gigs away from the big-time" apparently

Marlee: and he's convinced Gi that she can sing in the band so now she doesn't think she needs to care about her grades.

Marlee: they think they can spend all their time on their "art" and magically get famous from a youtube video they hope goes viral.

Jericho watched each of her texts come in succession, each one striking some nerve inside him. But the last one felt like a gut punch.

Does she really think that about artists?

He frowned, confused. He wasn't easily offended but for some reason, he felt insulted.

But he tried to ignore the feeling.

Jericho: sounds like they are just excited about what they do Mar

Marlee: which is fine but at some point, they have to think realistically

He stared at her message.

Realistically, huh?

His eyes shifted to his laptop and to what he thought had been an 'artfully inspired' post just moments ago. But in the half-hour, since he had posted it, there was only one like and a comment that was obviously from a bot.

He tried to change the subject.

Jericho: are you at least having a good time with your family?

Marlee: yeah, i've missed them <3

Marlee: but dude, thinking about g-money entertaining a guy like that in my old room!

Marlee: she's a smart girl, she could do so much better

Jericho suddenly felt sick to his stomach.

Jericho: right. Well i gtg see you tonight

Marlee: see you tonight! <3

Shoving his phone into his back pocket he tried to do the same with the sudden feelings of insecurity. But as he went about setting up and getting ready, and especially while he was waiting for six in the evening to come around, he couldn't quite shake them.

Hours later, while he was getting ready to leave, they were still nagging in the back of his mind.

Jericho fixed his nice suit jacket and brushed his dark hair away from his face.

She wasn't talking about you. Right? No. She wouldn't be supportive of my art otherwise.

He looked at the clock.

5:13 PM.

He was ready early, but that wasn't why he frowned. Marlee should have already been here by now. Checking his phone, there were no new messages. He decided that maybe she just hit traffic and sat on the edge of his bed waiting for her to call or show up.

And then twenty minutes went by and still— nothing.

Standing up, he knew he couldn't wait any longer for her, or he would be late for his debut. So, he grabbed his keys and left. When he arrived at the gallery, he checked his phone again.

Clicking on the messaging app an unread notification popped up from an hour ago.

He sighed.

I have got to get a different service provider.

He read the message.

Marlee: Flight changed; I'll be late!

His anxiety shot up a notch. He hoped that she wouldn't be too late. If she wasn't there to be his buffer, he was worried the conversations would fall flat.

Taking a breath, he got out of his truck and straightened his jacket.

I can do this.

◆ ◆ ◆

Standing next to a display of his own art was an ominous task for Jericho. He felt like bait for all of these tipsy strangers to meander over to and ask questions simply because he looked professional in his nice suit. Or because the paintings next to him grabbed their attention.

And though he was unprepared for how exposed he felt, there was a sliver of excitement that came with the interest of the viewers.

A few familiar faces showed up— August, Ada, Sanjay, and even Lena. And then it was back to trying to talk to strangers.

And Marlee still hadn't shown up.

"Your art style is beautiful, are you taking classes?" one older couple asked.

Jericho felt his heart racing in his chest even though it was a simple question.

"Thank you. Yeah, I am."

"Do you take on commissions?"

"Oh, no— no," he stammered, caught thinking about why he hadn't tried to take on commissions before this.

"More of a hobby, then?"

He could feel his face reddening.

"No, it's more than a hobby. Uh— I'll probably take commissions when I have more time for them."

Lame answer.

They nodded and continued to study his work before moving on. Jericho hated that it felt like if the viewers lost interest in him then they also lost interest in his art. He glanced nervously at the time again.

Where the fuck are you, Marlee?

After the last of the viewers had left, Jericho covered his

art with the protective sleeves he had brought. Then he sat on a table, yanking off his tie.

That was a bust.

It seemed like every conversation he had had that night ended in him stammering or fumbling his answers. And all he could remember were vague stares from the viewers, so the longer he thought about it the more he convinced himself that his work was unimpressive and bland.

He hadn't checked his phone again since about halfway through the night. It started buzzing on the table behind him but he didn't even glance at it.

He wrapped his tie around his hand, undid it, then rewrapped it over and over while he thought over everything he had said and analyzed each response or facial expression.

So when the doors opened and footsteps approached he didn't look up. And when a familiar voice called out to him, he was so frustrated with everything that he didn't want to meet her eyes.

Her wine-colored vans came into view.

"Jerry?"

His hands stilled, but he still didn't look at her— afraid she would see all of the emotions that were bubbling just under the surface.

Jericho didn't want to fight but he was tired of feeling like he wasn't enough or that his dreams and aspirations were somehow smaller than those with louder, clearer voices.

"Jerry, I'm so sorry I—"

He closed his eyes, interrupting her, "You promised you would be here."

"I know." Her voice was quiet— sounded like she had come closer.

"I *needed* you."

He hated that he felt so angry and hurt— hated that his eyes burned. But he was too spent from the day to put it aside.

"I'm sorry."

"Where were you?" he asked, finally looking up at her.

She tugged at the sleeves of her oversized sweatshirt.

"Things got intense talking to Gianna and I was late to my flight, so they had to move me to a new one," she explained.

"Intense? I thought you had the whole weekend to talk?" he didn't even care that he sounded snappy.

Her face reddened, glancing at some of the other artists that were still gathering their things.

"We did, but she wasn't listening to us. So, we tried to sit her down to try and convince her she's making a mistake."

"Making a mistake dating the loser artist, you mean."

She stared at him, her brows drawing together. She brushed some of the curls that had escaped her messy bun away from her face.

"That's not— I didn't mean— He's trying to distract her from her school. Before she met him, she wanted to be a lawyer. I can't just let her throw that away, Jerry."

"Let her? Can she not make decisions for herself?"

"Not if they're stupid! I'm her big sister, it's my job to look out for her."

"You can't control everything around you, Marlee. She's seventeen. Seventeen-year-olds make mistakes, that's how they grow," he argued, trying to keep his voice down.

She crossed her arms, chewing her lip as she looked away from him. Then she started shaking her head.

"I know you're upset I didn't make it back here in time, and I'm sorry— but you don't have to chew me out about it. I tried to get on an earlier flight, but they were full. There wasn't much I could do about it," she retorted.

"I don't know, you could have left well enough alone. Instead, you decided to host an intervention. Because—" he made air quotes— "'She's a smart girl, she could do so much better'."

She made a face.

"What's with the air quotes?"

"Were you telling Gianna she could do better or were you

just projecting because you can't stand having a lazy, loser artist for a boyfriend?"

Marlee's head tilted, looking incredulous.

"Jericho— what are you talking about? I have spent all today fighting to get here. I argued with airline... People— workers to get on a new flight. I freaking harassed a lady to switch tickets with me or a seat— anything. I still smell like airplane!"

She pinched her sweatshirt hem and pulled at it.

"I didn't even have time to change before I got here. Because I *wanted* to be here," she told him, her voice cracking as she looked on the verge of frustrated tears. "Why the hell would I go through all of that if I thought you were a loser?"

Jericho wanted to believe that, but after the day he had, he could only shrug and ran a hand through his hair.

"I don't know— maybe—"

"You're not a loser," she interrupted.

He glanced at his now-covered paintings and the stack of cards that he had spent hours designing with his contact information, Instagram account— anything that someone interested in his work would need to find him.

The leftover stack was disappointing to look at.

"If the gallery is any indication, I just might be."

"Jerry—"

"You know what, I'm tired," he sighed, standing up and draping his tie around his neck. "I just want to go home and sleep. I'll call you later."

And he was glad she didn't try to follow him as he carried his things out to his truck because he didn't think he had the energy to keep fighting.

CHAPTER TWENTY-NINE

Marlee

The entire week since their fight, Marlee felt like she was going a little crazy. She was trying to give Jericho his space, but she had gotten so used to his presence that when he wasn't around, it felt like there was something missing from her.

And then the last theater class before opening night rolled around and he didn't show up. Logically, she knew it was because the set design crew had no other work to do but it still felt personal. She couldn't help but think that if the day of the gallery had gone right, he would have shown up anyways to watch and be her silent encourager.

After that, when he still hadn't called, she started to feel sick to her stomach. She obsessively watched Pride and Prejudice, just hoping he would knock on the door and ask her to talk.

When Ada asked if she was okay, she just cried. And cried. She felt stupid about it because she'd never acted like this after a breakup. If that's what it was. That was what made it worse—that she didn't know if he still wanted to be with her.

But it was opening night and she had to suck it up.

The show must go on.

And the scout was still coming.

Glancing in the bathroom mirror, she touched up her red

lipstick and made sure the two silver pins were still securing one side of her curls up. Doing a half turn she smoothed her hands down over the cashmere-colored, silky material of her dress. Taking in a deep breath, she took a moment to slowly breathe out before exiting into the chaos of backstage.

Bennet, with the beast mask under his arm, smiled at her.

"Hey, boss!"

Sasha was busy making last-minute stitches in Talia's belle apron.

Marlee squeezed her friend's arm.

"How are you feeling?"

Talia grinned, her dark eyes lighting up.

"Like I'm gonna puke."

"Perfect," Marlee snorted. "Break a leg, people!" she called to the rest of the cast and headed for the auditorium.

It would be better to make some of the rounds now instead of trying to talk to everyone right after the show, she decided.

And hopefully, Jericho will show up.

Though, she wouldn't blame him if he didn't. It would be fair, considering she missed his gallery debut. But she was still hoping.

Weaving through the crowds of people, Marlee greeted familiar faces and other attendees— thanking them for coming. And all the while, her eyes scanned for Jericho.

But she didn't see him.

Trying not to feel discouraged, she told herself that he would show up at some point.

"Mar!"

Pausing, she turned to see Ada waving at her from where the group of her friends had seated themselves. Her smile got a little brighter. Excusing herself from another group of people, she headed in their direction.

"Hey! You guys are here," she said, hugging Ada, then August and Sanjay.

Looking behind them, she tilted her head.

"No Adler?"

Ada shook her head.

"He said to tell you 'break your back, or whatever theater kids say'," she laughed with a roll of her eyes. "He had a game tonight."

Marlee smiled.

"I'll have to tell him 'good try' later."

August looked around now, his thick brows quirking upward.

"No Jerry?"

"Uh, no, haven't seen him," Marlee told him, heat suffusing her neck.

"Weird, I saw him leave earlier... I thought he was headed here," he commented. Marlee just shrugged as her stomach dropped.

He probably went anywhere but here.

Sanjay glanced between them.

"I'm sure he'll be here soon."

Ada nodded and reached for Marlee's hand.

"Don't worry about it, tonight is gonna be great."

"Thanks."

Marlee wished that would have made her feel less like she was going to cry. Taking a breath, she straightened her shoulders.

"Glad you all could make it. I'll see you afterward, yeah?"

They all nodded and then walked around the auditorium again. Her eyes wandered but there was still no sign of Jericho. A glance at the clock told her it was only thirty minutes until curtains went up, so she made her way backstage again.

She pulled at her fingers and then at the ends of her curls.

"Thirty minutes until curtains, everyone!" she called out, not quite over the buzz of everyone chattering.

Clapping her hands to get their attention, Marlee repeated the information when everyone looked her way, "Thirty minutes— curtains go up! Let's do this, guys."

The door leading to backstage opened and Mr. Emery walked through. He waved at everyone, a clipboard under his arm.

Marlee waved, moving toward him.

"I'm excited to see what you and everyone else have accomplished Ms. Firth-Diaz," he said, adjusting his metal-framed glasses.

"I know they will blow your mind, Mr. Emery. Everyone has worked so hard."

Talia came over, hooking her arm through Marlee's.

"Marlee's been working hard too."

Mr. Emery smiled as he looked around at the costumes and set pieces that were arranged in neat and easily accessible patterns to make set and costume changes easy.

"I can see that. Good luck everyone. Tonight, counts as seventy percent of your final grade. Break a leg and you will see those grades in your inboxes no later than Wednesday."

With that said, Mr. Emery left, and the buzz started up again.

In a flurry of sequences that Marlee felt blended together, her cast asked her questions. The set crew confirmed details with her and the tech lead, of course, presented a problem to her with the microphones.

"Chad, do I look tech-savvy to you?" she asked, trying not to snap.

He blinked at her. "Uh—"

"Go ask Brett! He knows how to fix these issues, not me."

She shooed him out.

Bennet tapped her shoulder.

"Marlee, Mrs. Potts is throwing up."

"Oh, my— where is she?"

Marlee grabbed a water bottle and Bennet's sleeve. He took her back to the small bathroom next to the dressing room.

"Thanks," she said to Bennet and let him go as she knocked on the door.

"Uhm, Maddie? Can I come in, it's Marlee."

The door unlocked and Maddie peeked out, her face pale.

"I don't think I can do this."

"Yes—" Marlee moved into the bathroom and shut the door, trying not to sound panicked.

"Yes, you can. Here."

She handed her the water.

"Just sit down here and drink some water and breathe. I'll come to get you before you go on and you'll be great. I promise."

Maddie didn't look too sure, but she did as Marlee said.

"Okay..."

"Okay," she repeated with an encouraging smile.

And then she left to make sure the cast was ready for the opening act.

◆ ◆ ◆

Thankfully, Mrs. Potts stopped throwing up and was ready to go on by the time her first appearance rolled around. Marlee was thankful for that. And also, very thankful that, so far, there were only minor hiccups.

Easy fixes.

But she still chewed her nails as her eyes kept wandering out over the crowd. She told herself she was looking for the scout, but, really, she just wanted to see Jericho sitting out there.

The more times she looked the worse the pit in her stomach got. By the time Talia and Bennet started singing 'Something There', her eyes started burning. And all of a sudden, she wasn't seeing the production. Instead, memories of her and Jericho's stolen glances, laughing while they line-danced, and the smile lines that always appeared when he grinned ran through her mind.

She sniffed, quickly wiping away a tear.

God, I miss that smartass.

She smiled a little, but it quickly went away.

One of her cast members came off the stage, grinning at

her. She tried to smile back, laughing a little awkwardly and hoping they thought she was crying over the production.

Talia danced off stage next as the curtains were closing on the scene. Her cheeks were bright pink.

"How'd I do, Boss?"

Marlee blinked, shaking herself out of her thoughts. She felt horrible because she hadn't really been watching, but she knew Talia was one of the most talented actors on that stage, so she nodded.

"As always, you were a dream. Good job."

Talia's smile brightened, if it were possible, and she scurried off. Marlee looked back at the stage where the crew was quickly assembling the next backdrop. She realized that the crowd was still clapping for Talia and Bennet's performance. Pride swelled in her chest.

I just need to focus on this performance. Afterward, I'll find him, and we can talk.

Focusing was tough, but Marlee threw herself into every task and silly question directed at her. She cheered on her crew. Laughed with them and made sure they were drinking water.

By the end of the last act, Marlee clasped her hands to her chest and almost cried over how beautiful the entire thing was.

The clapping and cheering rang in her ears and her cheeks hurt from smiling as the cast took their last bow of the night.

We did it.

She started to grin, even more, thinking immediately that she wanted to hug Jericho.

Right.

She sobered. But Marlee was still over the moon about the performance on her cast and crew had put on.

CHAPTER THIRTY

Marlee

It had taken forever to get out of backstage. After making sure she had congratulated everyone and handed out the cards she had put together as a 'thank-you' for their hard work, Marlee ventured out into the crowd of attendees that were enjoying punch and talking loudly.

People congratulated her, and her friends waved at her, but she didn't have a chance to get to them before a lady dressed in a pressed pantsuit approached her. And in her gut, she knew she was the scout. Her heart rate picked up.

This is the moment.

She took a steadying breath.

Stay cool. Stay cool. Stay cool—

"Ms. Firth-Diaz?" The scout smiled, holding out a well-manicured hand for her to shake.

Marlee took her offered hand, praying that her own wasn't as sweaty as it felt.

"Yes, nice to meet you . . .?"

"Jessamine," she answered and let go of Marlee's hand. "Pleasure is mine. That was a beautiful performance. You should be proud."

Marlee tried not to smile too big, but she was still blushing.

"Thank you, everyone worked very hard."

"I would say so. Keep it up and you'll go places."

She waited for the rest of that sentence, but it never came as the scout glanced at her watch.

"Well, it was great to meet you, and, again, great job tonight."

And then she left.

Marlee felt like she had just gotten the wind knocked out of her lungs.

If anyone said anything to her, she didn't hear them as she made her way for the doors.

I need some air. I need to breathe... I need Jerry.

She could feel the burning in her eyes again. All she wanted was a hug and to hear him ask, 'You good?' so that she could let out the tears she refused to let fall in front of anyone else.

The cool night air felt amazing after being in the stuffy auditorium, and she finally felt like she could breathe. But now, outside, there were no people close by to help her forget his absence. Hugging her arms to her body, she rubbed her arms and walked a few steps in the direction of the studio.

She stopped.

He had pointed out how she felt the need to control everything around her and she didn't want to push him further away by trying to talk to him before he was ready.

Moving to the bench that sat in front of a small fountain, she sat down. Thinking over the conversation with the scout and then the fight with Jericho, she started to realize something.

She had been so quick to drag Gianna's boyfriend for wanting to be a one-hit-wonder picked up by producers on youtube and here she was with the same mentality. At her first production, she had thought the scout would come and be amazed— opening the doors to her Broadway career.

I guess I was projecting. But not about Jerry being a loser artist. I guess I should have been more realistic, she thought, pinching her fingers together as the tears pooled at her lashline.

There was no holding them back now.

"That was breathtaking."

Startled, Marlee straightened, wiping at her tears as she turned toward the voice, she had been waiting to hear all night. Seeing him there in his suit and that stupid cowboy hat made her heart dance in her chest.

But she didn't know if she should smile or not yet.

"Jerry," she said softly.

He stepped closer, looking down at his feet for a moment before meeting her eyes again.

"As a fan of Beauty and the Beast that was. . . I mean, I saw it at all the stages but seeing you pull it all together like that?"

The gentle smile that lifted the corner of his mouth almost made her cry again.

"You really pulled off something special, professor."

"You saw the whole thing?" She blinked, wondering how she didn't spot him in the crowd.

Especially in that hat.

He nodded.

"I didn't think you would show up. I wouldn't have blamed you if you didn't," she told him.

"Nah, I couldn't miss this. Besides, I put too much work into it."

She nodded, starting to smile a little bit because she agreed and was proud of him for it. Not just the work he did but putting up with her at the beginning.

"You're set design was ingenious."

He smiled back and took his hat from his head, holding the brim. There was a pause and then he looked at his feet and so did Marlee.

"Let me just. . .," he laughed nervously and cleared his throat. "First, I must tell you I've been the most unmitigated and comprehensive ass," he quoted, but she knew he meant the words.

She laughed, trying not to cry again.

"Jerry—"

"How— how could I ever make amends for such behavior."

Stepping a little closer, she quoted back to him the words that she also meant very much, "It is *I* who should be making amends." Shyly holding out her hand to him she asked, "Can we talk now?"

He took her hand, intertwining their fingers.

"Please."

◆ ◆ ◆

Jericho

Unlocking the door to the studio, Jericho and Marlee walked in and shut it. He looked over at the pillows that were still there from the last time they were here together, and he had been painting her portrait. The night after the gallery, he couldn't sleep and had come back to the studio with it. And since he had been worked up, he had only been able to face the painting for a few moments before he had locked up and left.

I never got to show her...

Gently, he tugged at her hand, and she followed quietly. There had been so many times he had almost called her or gone straight to her dorm to apologize and talk. Jericho hadn't missed a girl like he had Marlee.

Everything he did and everywhere he went reminded him of her. But it took him a while to work through all of the things he had been feeling and he hadn't wanted to talk to her until his mind was clear on those things.

Bringing her to the pile of pillows that were next to the easel still holding his painting of her, he paused. She brushed her hair behind her ear, her amber eyes seeming to search his face.

And then her eyes followed where he glanced— at the portrait of her drenched in watercolor.

Her lips parted slightly as her eyes bounced between him and the painting. He watched as she bit her lips together and her eyes turned glossy.

But before he could say a word, she was already apologizing.

Her thumb brushed along his as her voice cracked, "Jerry, I'm sorry for the way I acted and the things I said."

"You were just looking out for Gianna because she's important to you."

"I shouldn't have gotten so involved with Gi's decisions, it wasn't my place," she admitted. "You're important to me too, you know? The gallery was my idea in the first place and, dammit, I should have been there—"

"But you tried and did everything in your power to get back to me, and I shouldn't have gotten on your ass about it. I just let everything get to me," he told her, setting his hat on her head with a soft smile.

Marlee's cheeks turned pink, grabbing his wrist with her free hand.

"You? My head was so far up my ass, I couldn't see how hard I was projecting. I *was* the loser 'artist' thinking she would get her big break after one show."

His eyes softened and she sighed, "Honestly, I should have known better than to say those things." He laughed under his breath. Her fingers moved down his wrist to hold his other hand.

"And you're not a loser artist, Jericho. I've never thought that about you."

During their time apart, he had come to that realization but hearing her affirm it was still good for him to hear.

"I guess I should have known better too."

Her voice quieted, her eyes shining in the moonlight that filtered through the window, "Can we be in love again?"

There was a rush of butterflies that went through him at her words. Instead of answering, he tilted his head and leaned in to kiss her. Her eyes closed, kissing him back softly.

He pulled back just a breath and her eyes opened, dancing with his as she whispered, "Is that a, yes?"

Letting go of her fingers, his hand lifted to brush his thumb over her bottom lip.

"That's a *hell* yes," he answered quietly.

EPILOGUE

Jericho's larger handprint overlapped Marlee's on the canvas as his hand pressed to it. A swirl of bright pink and navy blue smeared over her neck as his other hand slipped behind it, their breathing coming as hard and fast as his thrusts.

Her paint-stained hands gripped his ribcage, lifting her legs higher on his hips to pull him deeper. And as he drove in, she bit down on his shoulder to muffle her moaning.

The mild sting only added to Jericho's pleasure. His muscles were starting to shake already. Turning his lips against her ear, he slowed his rhythm. And the slow movements only made her make more noise— biting harder.

"Fuck," he rasped. "You take me so well."

Another deep, slow thrust earned an almost musical moan from her.

"God, the sounds you make are so pretty."

She couldn't quite form a response as each move he made and every word he said ignited her. But when Jericho moved so he could see the blazing amber of her eyes again, her hands moved up to his shoulders to pull him close.

Looking into his eyes, she bumped her nose with his. Their breathing was almost synced.

Marlee lifted her chin and brushed a heated kiss to his lips, murmuring, "I love you."

"I love you," he echoed, his thumb pressing against her pulse.

Dragging kisses along her jaw and down her neck, Jericho admired all the strokes of color on her skin and the messy handprints.

"You're my favorite canvas," he groaned.

And then his momentum picked up again.

A smile flickered over her lips as she replied in a soft, breathless voice, "And you're my favorite artist."

He smiled back, resting his forehead against hers— so close she could see the blush on his cheekbones underneath the splatters of paint. And as their eyes connected Marlee tumbled into her orgasm, pulling him right with her.

Left breathing hard from rolling around in the paint, she could hardly catch her breath. Her fingers left messy prints on either side of Jericho's face as her hands lovingly moved up and down his back.

Jericho glanced at the canvas beneath them.

"That was messy," he teased even though it had been his idea.

She giggled, trying to wipe away some paint from his shoulder. But she only succeeded in making more of a mess since her fingers were also very colorful.

"I got carried away with the paint— too many colors."

Jericho's smile softened, resting his elbow on the canvas. He used his thumb to brush through the turquoise on her temple, the pink on her bottom lip, and the navy blue at her neck.

His eyes lifted to hers again.

"Nah, I don't think so."

His fingers swirled through the maroon paint over her heart.

"I love *all* your colors."

ACKNOWLEDGEMENT

I'll keep it short and sweet because I know most people don't read these. Thank you to Isaac, Joy, and Courtney for your help with this project. From catching grammar mistakes to being excited about this little story as much as I was- you kept me writing. I appreciate you so very much.

And to my husband for putting up with my late night rants and the incessant clacking of my type writer keyboard. But always cheering me on and the occasional shoulder rubs while I was stressing.

Lastly, a shout out to Pepsi for keeping me going during writing sessions.

ABOUT THE AUTHOR

Kylie R. Trask

Kylie R. Trask is a small-town girl who grew up with a love for stories. Storytelling from a young age grew into a passion. She published her first book in 2020, 'Dream Catcher: The Exile', and it has since been turned into an audiobook. She has plans for many new books. She and her husband have two beautiful kids, and when Kylie isn't creating stories, they like to relax and game together.

www.ingramcontent.com/pod-product-compliance
Lightning Source LLC
LaVergne TN
LVHW041211150826
845673LV00001B/353

* 9 7 9 8 3 7 1 4 0 1 8 0 9 *